KING

By Alana Keli'ipule'ole Trumbo

Edited by Alexis Cotant

CHAPTER 1

Emmett

You know the say no to drug weeks we would have in school? It was one of the ribbons week, I can't remember which color it was. I always told myself, I would never end up like the people they told us about.

I was always the smartest kid in my classes, so no one would have guessed that I would end up doing what I do. But when you have a kid brother at home, crying from hunger pains and no idea where your mom went, you have to do what you have to do.

I know, a sob story about how I became the man I am, but I don't regret it one bit. My brother got into college and I was able to help him pay for it. To him, he thinks that I have always been a hard working mechanic.

That isn't a complete lie, but owning a mechanic shop is not how I could pay for his education which consists of drinking and fucking whoever he can. He swears that this is how college is like and that I would understand if I ever finished high school.

If that boy actually knew what I had to do for him, he wouldn't be making jabs about my lack of an education.

Since we are the only family that each other has, we have a weekly dinner that I don't let anyone or anything make me miss.

Eating at a restaurant seemed like a pipe dream when we were growing up. Which is why I make the effort to take my brother to dinner at least once a week and to stock his fridge with whatever he needs.

I'm the closest he is getting to a father.

Mom swears she has no idea who his father is, but I guess that's better than the guy who I share half of my genes with. However, that didn't stop his 'father' from stomping back into his life once Logan was all grown.

Logan and I could not look any more different, you wouldn't even know we were related if it wasn't for the fact that we fight like brothers.

It is more than the fact that I am covered in tattoos, and he has none. He has light brown hair, almost blonde and green eyes, whereas I have dark hair and blue green eyes. Our builds have always been the same, it probably has to do with the fact that we didn't have that much food around growing up. Now that I make sure that we are both always fed, we have more of a muscular build.

It is like the before and after for Captain America, we are now in the after stage.

"Hurry up, dipshit! I'm hungry!" I yell out of my car as Logan takes his sweet time talking to some girl outside of his apartment door. It isn't the first time I have caught him with a girl, but at least this time they are both fully dressed.

Logan holds up a middle finger to me, but that doesn't stop me from honking. I gotta be a cockblock somehow.

He runs over to me with that look like he needs a favor. I know this look very well.

"You think we can give my friend a ride home? Her car is in the shop and I'm really trying to sleep with her." Logan hangs on the open window.

"Don't hang on my door. I just got it fixed from the last time you borrowed my car." I scold. This boy really borrowed my car and scratched the doors on god's know what. My car is the closest I have to a baby, it's my subie. A Subaru Impreza is the car I dreamed of having, but didn't ever think it would be a reality. So, yes I am hard on Logan on how he treats it. "Yeah, but this does mean I'm choosing where we are going for dinner."

"Not Korean BBQ again, I hate doing all the cooking." He whines before turning to the girl and giving her the nod that I said it was okay. Logan goes to open the passenger seat for himself.

"Who fucking raised you? Give the girl the front seat."

"I'm not riding in the back, like I'm a child." Logan complains, but he listens and gets into the back. He is too tall for the back since the passenger seat is pushed back pretty far along with the driver seat. It is the curse of us both being over 6 feet tall.

"I'll stop treating you like a child when you stop acting like one." I look into the rearview mirror, quietly laughing about the image. His knees to his chest and the amount he has to slouch, so I can still see around his big ass head. "Maybe if you are good and eat all of your dinner, you can have dessert."

"Blake, this is my annoying older brother Emmett. Emmett, this is my classmate Blake." Logan introduces us. Blake isn't like a girl that he would typically go after, she is beautiful.

I'm not saying he doesn't go after beautiful girls, but this one is breathtakingly beautiful. The kind of girl that makes you stop and wonder how you were blessed with the presence of an angel.

She smelled like vanilla, I could smell that the second she got inside. It wasn't an overpowering smell, but more of a luring in one.

"I'm sorry for interrupting your family dinner. My car was supposed to be done today, but I don't know what's taking so long. I just live behind the liquor store on 3rd." Blake admits, staring down at her lap. Her red hair was hanging in front of her face.

I know exactly where she lives, it is the trailer parks that Logan and I once lived in. I got us out of there, it took heaven and hell but I did it.

"Which mechanic did you take your car to?" Logan asks from the backseat, I was wondering the same thing. There are only two in this town, including my own shop. So, unless she took it to a different town, I have an idea of which one she took it to.

"I don't know the name, it was the one on Maple." She looks up from her hands and out the window. She's closer to Logan's age than mine, so I shouldn't be sitting here and thinking about how beautiful she looks. How much I want to reach out and brush her hair out of her face.

I haven't been with a girl in close to 10 years. It isn't like I haven't had girls wanting to be with me. It is that there came a time where my life was too dangerous to have someone else. That's why I pay for Logan to have an apartment, away from me when I have a big enough house for the both of us.

After a while it became easy not to think about women, when I have Logan to take care of.

"Emmett owns a mechanic shop, so maybe he can call and see what the hold up is." Logan is ahead of me. I was planning on doing that, but not to help Logan. No, for my own selfish reasons.

I'm too fucking old for her, I shouldn't be sitting here thinking about her when Logan so obviously wants her.

I would do anything for Logan, even give up my own happiness for him.

CHAPTER 2
Blake

"Was that the Thornton boys?" My grandma sits near the window with Jeopardy on the TV playing on max volume. It took some getting used to in the last two years, but it's nice to be with her.

After my parents died, she didn't complain or say that I was almost 18, so I didn't need an adult to take care of me. She had some neighborhood boys clean out her craft room and turned it into my bedroom.

"Oh yeah, Logan and I have a project together." I look inside the fridge to find dinner nicely wrapped for me. A downside of living with your grandma, she eats dinner at 6 pm while I was at Logan's trying to convince him to let me do all the work.

I hate partner projects or group work or whatever you want to call it.

I always tell the person I will do all the work and put their names on it. I can typically guarantee them an 'A' which is why they usually agree.

Logan on the other hand, would not take my deal. I thought when I got paired with Beta Alpha Alpha Kappa President, he was going to say yes.

I actually have no idea what the name of his frat is or if he is in one, but he gives me those vibes.

"You should stay away from them." My grandma says as the credits for Jeopardy plays, which is her que for bed. "They aren't good kids. That older one is bad news."

"You think every boy is bad news." I pop open the microwave right when 1 second is left on it making it so there was no beep. It is a sign of accomplishment and because I have gotten used to tiptoeing around past 8 pm.

"Blake, I'm serious about this one."

My grandma is sweet and rarely has to lay down the law with me. Ever since I moved in with her, she has let me be.

When I came to her, I was a mess, locking myself away in my room. I didn't even want to talk to her and she would leave food for me outside of my door, not forcing me to talk or do anything.

Then one day, I took my plate to the table with her and we ate in silence.

I wouldn't be alive if it wasn't for her.

CHAPTER 3
Emmett

"Come on James, why are you trying to hustle this girl out of her money?" I say into the phone, I knew exactly what James was doing. He takes forever on a project and says that it was worse than he expected, so he can charge more.

"Emmett, I don't come into your shop and criticize you for selling molly to every single customer and you don't come into my shop and criticize how I run it." James says.

James and I have always had this hard relationship, it is because I hate how shady his business is. But I guess you could say the same about my business.

"How much for you to let me take the car?"

"700."

"700?! You piece of shit. 500." I counter. I am so close to driving over there and beating the living shit out of James.

"650."

"575 and I'll have one of my boys drop something off for you." I know that James has a drug of choice, almost everyone does. Once you know what it is you can use that to your advantage.

"Deal."

"Teddy, get the truck and pick up a car from that fuckers shop." I slam the phone down, yelling over the loud sounds of my shop. We are the only shop within 75 miles that will work on luxury cars, so we are in high demand.

"You know I hate going there." Teddy rolls his eyes, pulling his baseball cap lower as he gets out of the car he was detailing.

"Did I ask if you would like to go? Or did I tell you to fucking go?" I hate repeating myself with some of these dipshits. If it is a lack of knowledge that is one thing, but when it comes to this.

"Fuck, sorry boss." He quickly apologizes, grabbing the company card and a sack from me.

If Teddy didn't look young enough to not look suspicious at a rave, I would have fired him long ago. He's a shit mechanic and an even dumber person.

That's why he's only on detailing, a mind numbing task for a mind numbing person.

~~~~

Blake's car is older than dirt and drives like it too. The amount of lights on her dashboard that are lit up makes it look like a Christmas tree.

I'm surprised her car hasn't blown up.

She doesn't deserve to drive this piece of trash. But I can't just upgrade her car. I don't know this girl. She doesn't know me.

Yet, I want to know her.

I haven't felt this way about a girl since high school.

Logan wants her though, it doesn't mean she wants him. But I can't do that to him.

I've spent my whole life trying to help him, trying to make his life better. I can't steal the girl he wants. It wouldn't be right.

But I can give her a drivable car even if it means I have to strip this car to barebones and rebuild it myself. I can do that for her.

CHAPTER 4

Blake

A number I don't recognize comes across the screen. It's been a week without my car and taking the bus everywhere has not been ideal.

My grandma doesn't drive anymore because her eyes are too far gone, so it was her car that I used. But it sat in the driveway for far too long that it has so many problems.

I ignored most of it because I didn't have the money to fix it. I still don't have the money, but I had no choice. Even with working overtime at a coffee shop and waitressing, I don't think I'll have enough to pay the mechanic.

Mom and dad left behind some money as part of the life insurance, but I can't use it until I graduate college. It was a hidden clause. They really didn't expect to die before I graduated college.

"Blake?" The deep masculine voice asks.

"This is her." I answer.

"Hey Blake, it's Emmett. Logan's brother. I just finished up your car. Logan or I could come get you so you can pick it up." His voice sounded happier, more uplifting.

He looked nothing like Logan, which was surprising. I couldn't believe that this hunk of a man was giving me a ride home. But he would never go for a girl like me.

I have far too many issues. Double whammy with me, mommy and daddy issues. I guess that's what happens when you lose your parents unexpectedly.

"Oh fuck. I'm out of classes at noon, but I have work at 1:00 so I can't pick it up today."

"Where do you work?"

"The Chili's on main." I answer.

"It'll be there waiting for you."

He doesn't let me tell him no, that he doesn't need to go out of his way for me or anything like that.

~~~~

"Blake, there is some hot tattooed guy asking to sit in your section? I can lie and say you just went to lunch, if you don't want him to know you are here." The hostess Claire asks. Her coming to find me kind of gave me away that I was here. If he was an actual stalker and not Logan's hot older brother, then this is not the way to go.

"No, you can sit him in my section." I look over at the tattooed man, who looks out of place in this family establishment.

"Hi! I'm Blake. I'll be your waitress this evening. Is there anything you would like to start off with? Drinks or an appetizer?" I do my usual spiel trying not to let him know how nervous he actually makes me.

"Can I just start off with whatever IPA you have on tap?" Emmett smiles, making me melt.

"Yes, can I just get a quick look at your ID?"

"It's been a while since I've been carded. But anything for you. And Logan will be joining me soon, he just got out of some frat meeting." Emmett pulls his wallet out of his back pocket and shows me his ID.

32.

CHAPTER 5
Emmett

I should have left the key on the tire or just dropped the key off with the hostess. But then I saw her, the way her curvy body was being shown off with her fitted uniform and apron. I then heard her voice and all of a sudden I'm texting Logan that we are having dinner at Chili's.

This is not a safe location for her to be working at. The alley behind here is where many deals go down.

I can't believe she was taking public transportation to this place. She is a nice girl, she is an easy target.

I was once the one doing the targeting, so I know what they are looking for.

"I'll get that IPA right to you." Blake nervously hands me back my ID. Why am I going after a girl who could be a decade younger than me? If I'm this hellbent on dating a girl I should find someone my age instead of going after someone Logan wants.

"I didn't know that Blake worked here." Logan takes the seat across from me, pulling me out of my thoughts. "Caleb is going to get me after dinner. Betas are throwing a party, so we are pregaming at his."

"Did you get that paper done?" I go to look through the menu as if Chili's hasn't had the same menu for my whole life.

"What the fuck, Emmett? Can we have one meal where you don't act like my father? You aren't my father."

"Yeah, I'm better than either of our fathers. I actually stuck around for you. So, yeah I am going to sit here and ask if you have finished your paper because I am the one who is paying for your education and your apartment and making sure you have money, so you can go to stupid parties and pregame." I snap. It has been a while since Logan and I have gotten into an argument. I think I can still take him in a fist fight if need be.

"I don't need you to do any of that for me. I can take out student loans and work. How hard could it be?" Logan says like the privileged boy he has got to be thanks to me.

"You are so goddamn spoiled. I wanted to give you everything that I didn't have growing up. And you want to throw it all away because you are throwing a hissy fit?"

His jaw clenches with anger. "I'm tired of you controlling my life, Emmett." Storming out of the restaurant, he leaves me.

Even after all these years, he still wants his bio dad to have an actual relationship with him. I wrote my bio dad off when I was 12 and he tried to bum money off of me when I was stealing diapers and baby food for Logan. Like I had any spare money to give.

Logan's father left when our mom said she was pregnant, so he didn't meet him until he was 18. And somehow this man has made me the bad guy and said that I didn't let Logan have a relationship with him.

Which he uses that guilt to get money out of Logan. I have tried to talk to him about it, but he doesn't care. He has always wanted his father in his life, so he won't listen to me.

Eating alone isn't something new to me, so I wasn't going to let Logan ruin my dinner. I also was avoiding going back to my place.

It's Friday night, so my crew were picking up their supplies for all the parties. I had already given everything out, so it would be lonely.

It's the life I chose. I don't look young enough to be scooping out parties anymore, so I stay behind and handle the money and inventory.

Cops know who I am for my petty crimes from when I was a teenager, but they haven't been able to get me for dealing drugs. Upside of having the cops in your pocket.

"Get the fuck out of here!" I yelled at the guy who had Blake's car on bricks as he was stealing the last of her tires. I knew I shouldn't have gotten her new rims, this was my mistake. I made her a target.

"This fucking day!" Blake cries out, walking out seconds after I scared the guy away. This is why she shouldn't work on this side of town, it's dangerous. She could have easily been the one to catch him and no saying what he would have done.

"Blake, come on I can take you home, so I can pick up my tow truck and I'll put new tires on it for you." I offer. There was no question about it. I was going to fix her car. I don't know why, I want to help her so much. I want to be around her.

I didn't need to stay after Logan left me, but I did.

CHAPTER 6

Blake

I hate taking handouts, Emmett wouldn't let me pay him for the work he did already on my car. And then he left me a huge tip. I get that he thinks I am white trash given that I live in a trailer park, but I don't want his pity.

It is something I have dealt with my whole life, my mom got pregnant with me during high school. So, my dad went straight to work after graduating high school.

We never had a ton of money, which is probably why they never took out life insurance. I spent the first two years after their death paying back all their debts and the funeral expenses.

I couldn't put off going to college any longer, so working two jobs to afford my tuition is what I have to do.

"Emmett, I'm not taking another one of your handouts. I can afford to get my car fixed." That's a lie, but I can ask for an extension for my current tuition bill. I would prefer not to do that, but I need my car. "I don't need you looking down upon me."

"I'm not giving you a handout." Emmett snapped. "Blake, I'm not looking down on you. I won't accept your money for this."

"So, what? Prostitution?" I jokingly say. I would let Emmett fuck me for free, but he would never go for me. The way his muscles show through his flannel shirt as he tenses. I want him.

"N-no, n-no not that. I would never do that." Emmett stammers. I burst out in laughter watching him get so defensive. "Oh, you were joking. You can help me put the new tires on and we can consider that payment."

"I don't think me holding a flashlight for you would count as payment for all the work you have done."

"It's better than what you offered up. Because I know we take Apple Pay now, but I don't think we have listed sex as one of the payment options." He jokes.

"Well, you better get ahead of the curve and start offering it before Apple copyrights it and you miss out on millions." Am I really doing this? Joking about having sex with Emmett in the middle of a Chili's parking lot?

But as a virgin, I should really stop joking

about it because on the off chance he actually takes me up on it I won't be able to do.

It isn't like I don't know how to have to sex. I have watched porn, but I know that he would never want me.

Emmett

My dick really has a mind of itself because the moment she mentioned having sex, I felt all the blood rushing to it.

She deserves someone better than a high school dropout who runs a drug empire. I'm a loser.

I hold open the passenger side door of my Subie for her. I may not have had a father figure in my life, but I do know how to not act like a douche.

"You can play whatever you want." I hand her my phone with Spotify open. I figure she didn't want to listen to the audiobook I was in the middle of. I always liked English when I was in school and I was a big reader.

So, this is the only way I can still read since I am beyond busy.

"I don't think you will like the kind of music I like." She mutters, placing my phone in the center console.

"As long as you don't put on screaming yaks then we are good."

"What about screaming llamas?" Blake giggles, reaching for the phone again.

"That's actually all I listen to. So, you are speaking to the right man." I hate how easy it feels to be around her. I hate it because I don't deserve this nice of a girl to be in my life.

"I don't think you understand. That's ALL I listen to."

CHAPTER 7

Blake

My grandma hasn't asked why I came home so late last night and I was full of giggles. It's stupid, he could have any girl he could ever want, but I am giddy about him.

My phone dings with a text, my hands are covered in cookie dough as I was making a thank you gift for Emmett. He may not let me pay him, but he can't deny cookies.

"Hey Grandma, can you tell me what the text says?" I ask. She was sitting at the kitchen table reading a book for her book club. I think her book club is an excuse for them to get together and drink wine. But, I won't say anything.

"How do you turn it on?" She takes her readers off her head and puts them on her eyes. It would have been easier for me to wash my hands and read it.

"Just press the button on the side." I went to the sink to wash my hands as I rolled the last bit of cookie dough in the cinnamon sugar mixture. I don't know how many people he has in his shop, so I am hoping that I made enough for him.

"From someone named Logan English 201, he wants to know if you want to meet at his apartment again. Is this the boy you were out late with last night?" Grandma puts her readers back on top of her head. "This better not be Logan Thornton."

"Grandma, I told you I have class with him and he's my partner for this project. And no, I wasn't with anyone last night. I just got held up at work, a table that wouldn't leave and I still had to finish my side work." I lie. I hate lying to her, but if I told her I was alone with Emmett Thornton in his mechanic shop she would ground me.

"Just that Emmett boy is bad news. Slinging drugs and women, you should stay away from him. His mama still lives here and she is always high. She brings trouble to the neighborhood with the boys she brings away. I always told your mama not to hang out with her, but she didn't listen. And that's how she got knocked up with you. Thank god, she listened to me and left that guy. If it wasn't for your dad, she would have never made it out of here." My grandma inspects my cookies, as if I haven't been baking since I was old enough to be in the kitchen with her.

"Wait, what do you mean? I thought she

married my dad because *he* knocked her up." I stammer. My grandma is acting as if she did not drop earth shattering news to me.

"I thought they told you. I told them they couldn't keep that from you forever. All I know is your bio father found out that your mom was pregnant and gave her 500 dollars to 'take care of it' and to never contact him again. Your dad was always in love with your mom since kindergarten, so he stepped up for you two. Now, who are you making cookies for?" She stops the timer on the stove as I was still in shock over hearing this.

"Just for the shop that fixed my car."

I went on autopilot driving from my house to the mechanic shop, still in my head over the truth bomb that was dropped on me.

"Blake! Did someone mess with your car again?" Emmett greets me before I am even able to exit my car. He wipes his hands on a dirty washcloth before running over to me.

His work shirt hangs open with a white long sleeve underneath the collared shirt. The long sleeve covers most of his tattoos except his neck and hand pieces. The ones on his hands are probably my favorite of the ones that I can see, it's of the bones in his hand.

"No, I made cookies." I stammer, unable to

really think.

"You really didn't have to. Is everything okay?" He opens the door for me, offering a hand for me.

"If you found out that the guy who raised you wasn't biologically your dad, would that change anything for you?" I probably shouldn't be asking such a forward question to a guy I barely know, but I don't have anyone else to talk to.

"Here, let's go to my office." Emmett reaches over me and turns off my car as I wouldn't move and still had my hands on the wheel. He unbuckles my seatbelt and gently pries my hands off the wheel. "Mia, don't let Teddy break anything."

"You are really leaving Mia in charge of me! I deserve more than that." A younger looking guy with a baseball cap on, complains.

"Shut up Theodore, before I give you something to complain about." A beautiful girl emerges from under a car and throws something heavy at Teddy.

"Let's get to the office before we become witnesses to a murder." Emmett quickly leads me through a busy shop into a quiet office. His office lacks decorations, but not furniture. The walls of his office are filled with bookcases. There are more books in this small office than my whole house.

I sit awkwardly on the edge of the couch, kind of feeling like I am back in a therapist's office and not one of a hot tattooed mechanic.

"I'm sorry, we don't even know each other and yet I was just trauma dumping on you. I just found out something crazy today and you were the first person I saw." I immediately apologize before he even shuts the door. Emmett sits next to me on the couch, he once again holds his hand out for me. I want to take it, but I know all it will do is make me fall for him more. And he wouldn't want to be with me.

"Daddy issues are kind of my specialty, so you came to the right guy." Emmett places his hand on top of mine, trying to comfort me. "Did this man come back in your life and ask for money or something? Did your parents…"

"They're dead." I interrupt, like ripping off a bandaid. I find it easier to do it that way instead of tiptoeing around it.

"I'm sorry." He squeezes my hand, I give in and take my hand off my knee to let him hold. Emmett's hands are bigger than mine and rougher, but it feels right to let him hold it.

"I don't understand why people say sorry to me about that. Like you didn't cause the drunk driver to hit their car." In reality, it's my fault. They were coming home from dinner and I asked if they would stop and get me ice cream. My mom said no, that there was ice cream in the freezer. There wasn't, only popsicles, so my dad said yes they would stop. They died pulling out of the 7/11 parking lot.

The grief therapist that my grandma sent me to, said it's not my fault and I have to stop blaming myself. But how can I? I didn't need the ice cream.

"I think people are trying to be empathic with you." He rubs his thumb over the palm of my hand, the silver ring on his thumb is covered in grease.

"I really don't mean to dump all of this on you." I whisper. I haven't really had another person to talk to in so long.

I lost all of my friends who I moved two hours away to live with my grandma. I know that's not a far distance, but maybe it was my lack of contact as I was grieving the loss of them. But somewhere around month 6 or 7 they moved on without me.

"I did admit that I listen to screaming llamas, so it was your turn to admit a deep dark secret." He tries to make light of the situation, making me laugh a little. Emmett reaches up and wipes away the tears on my face. "Here I'll give you my phone number in case you feel the need to admit to listening to screaming goats or something like that, and I'm not at the shop."

CHAPTER 8

Emmett

I handed her a business card, a fucking business card with my personal cell phone number written on the back. If that doesn't show my age, then my god.

I know her number from when I had to call her from the shop's number, but it feels invasive and creepy to text her. I gave her my number, she will use it when she wants to.

It's been a couple days and I haven't heard from her. Which I should be happy about because then she doesn't need a shoulder to lean on.

But, I'm not. I want to go back and savor the moments I had with her in my office. I hated how I was covered in grease, so I couldn't hold her as she cried.

My office still smelled like the vanilla perfume she uses, hours after she left.

My black cat Crucio sits on his cat tree when I enter my house after a long day in the shop.

I know a Harry Potter name, but it was one of the first big chapter books that I read. But also, I thought Crucio was a good name because people think black cats are evil.

I originally went to the shelter to adopt a dog, but this black cat would not leave me alone. A member of the staff had let him out of his cage, so he could roam for a couple hours. They said he's usually really shy and hides underneath their desk.

But the moment I walked in, he wouldn't leave my legs alone. I knew that I had to go home with this cat.

It does make this big house feel less lonely as I don't let Logan come over. I have to keep him safe from my lifestyle, so the further I keep him away the better.

Not going to lie, I didn't share a single cookie with my staff. And now I have a couple snickerdoodles left which I was going to save for after my workout.

I open the door to the garage and Crucio follows me out. He likes to just sit out there with me. When I first got him, I didn't let him follow me into the garage and he meowed at the door until I let him in.

I press play on the audio book that I was

listening to.

It's some contemporary fiction novel that just won an award. It was recommended for me by the app I use. But I haven't gotten super into it yet, this workout would be a good time for the book to hopefully pick up and captivate me.

Or else I'm going to have to relisten to Harry Potter and the Prisoner of Azkaban.

My phone vibrates with a text message before I even have a chance to do my first squat. I take it as a sign to take a minute before working out.

It's an unknown number and a badly photoshopped picture of an album cover for a band called 'Screaming goats'.

Emmett: Wow, a new album already. I was so moved by their first album. I don't know if I'm ready for this one.

Sent 9:56 pm

The three dots show up immediately as she goes to text me back.

Blake: I just hope they go on tour for this album. I need to get barricade for this. I may have to camp out for it.

Sent 9:57 pm

I chuckle. Logan told me to stay out of his life, so that means he can't be upset over Blake, right? That's what I have to tell myself as my thumbs quickly type out a new message.

Emmett: I guess we will have to camp out together bc I am going to get barricade as well. Maybe even VIP. Gotta meet the masterminds behind the album.

Sent 10:00 PM

Crucio meows as my phone vibrates again. I rerack my weights.

"Dean." I answer the phone. Dean is my right hand man, he looks much younger than me, so he can still work on the college campus.

"They got Teddy. We are on our way to yours. It's not good." Dean quickly explains and hangs up the phone. I rush inside, clearing off my dining room table, pulling out every piece of medical equipment that I have and a large bottle of vodka.

I don't know if it's for me or Teddy, but it's possible that we will both need it.

A bloody and bruised Teddy is carried in, I can barely recognize his face.

"Boss, they got my hat." Teddy groans in pain as Dean throws him on the table.

"I'll get you a new hat, you just can't die on me." I take a swig of the vodka before handing it over to Dean to sterilize the needle, so we can stitch Teddy up.

This is why I can't do anything with Blake. This life is too dangerous for her to be a part of.

CHAPTER 9

Blake

Maybe it was stupid of me to text Emmett. It was like he dropped off the face of the Earth. That last text I sent to him still says read, no text back.

I even borrowed my grandma's phone to see if my phone was receiving texts.

It was.

Work made a new rule that we had to park down the block after my tires were stolen. They don't want to be liable if something happens again to one of our cars.

So, instead at the end of the night we have to walk 10 minutes in the dark with all of our tips in our pocket.

We could easily get mugged, but they don't care if it means that we are not on their property.

Emmett shows across my phone as it vibrates in my hand, startling me. I think about sending it to voicemail, but talking to someone on the phone will make me feel better.

If I get mugged at least someone will know where to find my dead body.

Putting my earphones in my ears, I hit answer and slip my phone back in my pocket.

"Just like Jesus on day three you rose from the dead." I tease, but immediately regret it when I hear how tired his voice sounds.

"I have spent all day trying to figure out the best way to text you that I have had a whirlwind of the last couple days, so I haven't had a chance to talk and I wasn't ghosting you." Emmett's voice sounds sad and broken, most of all vulnerable.

"Everything okay? I have been told that I'm a good listener." I clutch the pepper spray in my hand tightly, looking around. This walk seems even longer since I had to stay late and roll silverware.

"Blake, where are you? Are you walking? It is almost midnight. Please tell me you did not just get off work. Is the car having issues again?" Emmett's sad voice turns to anger and concern.

"Yeah after my tires got stolen, they have us parking down on Hatch, so they aren't liable if something happens to us."

"That's a 15 minute walk. Why didn't you call me? I would have picked you up. You shouldn't walk that far at night! It's dangerous!" Emmett argues. How concerned he is makes my heart flutter. It's stupid, he is just acting this way because he is a good person.

Any good person would have this reaction.

"It's almost like you just rose from the dead. Remember? I didn't think you wanted to hear from me." I quietly admit.

"Blake Sanders, I always want to hear from you."

~~~~

And we spoke like that all night. I almost didn't wake up for my 5 am shift at the local coffee shop. But Emmett doesn't need to know that.

Emmett: Goodmorning. Do you work tonight?

Sent 5:15 am

Blake: Goodmorning! You are awake early, what kind of car problems happen this early? It's Friday night, so of course I'm working. Families gotta have their unlimited chips and salsa.

Sent 5:20 am

Emmett: No car problems at this time, just couldn't sleep. I'll be waiting outside for you.

Sent 5:21 am

CHAPTER 10
Emmett

I didn't know how to tell Blake that I was up so early because I hadn't slept yet.

Teddy lays out on my couch, I haven't sent him home yet because the first day was really touch and go. I didn't want to send him home until I knew for sure he wasn't going to die on us.

"When were you going to tell me that you are seeing Mia?" I place a plate of food in front of him. He had some more color to his face, so I am hoping that means he is on the up.

I never went to medical school, but I have learned a lot from books and from first hand experience. Once you get known as the guy who knows how to stitch people up, it gets around.

"She threatened to kill me if I told anyone as sleeping with me was something so horrible that she would rather be known as a murderer than someone willing to sleep with me." Teddy grunts as he tries to move. Luckily, they missed all of his vital organs, so it was just a lot of stitches to keep him from bleeding out.

"Well, the only reason she isn't here right now is because I sent her home to get some sleep. Her and I were taking turns to make sure you didn't stop breathing while you were in a drug induced sleep." I sat in the recliner that Mia and I had taken turns in during the last two days, one of us would sit here watching him while the other napped or shower or went to the bathroom. I may or may not have been pissing in bottles. Don't worry I threw them out, I'm not a heathen.

"Emmett, you really do have the good shit because I don't remember anything from the last two days." Teddy takes a small bite of the toast, doing basically anything for the next couple weeks will be painful for him. But I already put him in so much danger by dealing drugs, I refuse to let him become a pill popping addict.

I know a drug dealer with morals.

"Yeah, well you're back on over the counter drugs, so you better get ready to tough it out."

"Fuck man, well if you are going to be a hardass can you at least distract me from the pain? Like with who is that hot young redhead that came by the shop? I didn't take you as one who would want curves like that. I thought of you more of a Megan Fox type of man not a Kardashian." Teddy is really pushing it, I feel my jaw clench and my fists form.

"Remember I have your life in my hands." I sternly say, walking off to the kitchen to pour myself another cup of coffee. I'm not discussing Blake with Teddy, he doesn't deserve to hear about her.

~~~~

"You sure you will be okay watching him?" I ask Mia, Chili's closes in an hour and I live 40 minutes away. I would rather be sitting there waiting for her than for Blake to walk alone.

"Yeah, even before the injuries I overpowered him, so he is even easier to watch now." Mia jokes, she knows where I'm going. I didn't expect to open up to her about Blake, but during the late night neither one of us wanted to watch any more Netflix. She had opened up about Teddy, so I felt the need to. "Now, go see your girl."

"Just make sure Crucio doesn't escape." I stammer as Mia pushes me out the front door. She's a strong girl despite her short stature.

Sitting outside of a Chili's an hour after closing and listening to an audiobook is not where teenage me thought I would be. I never had anything to live for, so I thought once I had saved up enough money to set Logan up for success I would...

Never mind, let's not go there tonight.

"Emmett, I didn't think you were serious." Blake holds open the passenger side door, I press pause on the audio book.

"I told you I would be here. It is too dangerous to have you walking that far this late." I feel at peace knowing that she is safe in this car.

"That's why I bought this." She pulls out a pink and sparkly pepper spray holding it like a shiny new toy.

"Yes, because that will do a lot against a gun." I chuckle.

"You want me to test it out? You can be my first victim." Blake slyly smiles and holds it out, ready to spray me with it if it wasn't for the safety. The sparkle in her eye of pure joy. I fucking like this girl.

"Ahh take my wallet you can have it." I jokingly hold my hands up after parking the car behind hers.

"I'll let you off easy this time. Thanks for the ride, Emmett." Blake looks down at her lap, nervously.

"Do you work tomorrow night?" I ask, she nods. "I'll be here."

I don't mind if this is my life as long as she is a part of it. That's all I want.

CHAPTER 11

Blake

Emmett kept his promise, every single shift I would walk out and he would be waiting for me. Word got around and everyone knew that there would be a black subie, as he calls it, with an extremely attractive tattooed man waiting for me.

Not once did he complain when I would have a table that wouldn't leave and he would be waiting for 2 plus hours.

The 2 minutes it takes him to drive from the restaurant to my car never felt like enough time. He would listen about my shift, but never open up about his day as there was not enough time.

I was spending this particular day with a Thornton boy, but not the one I wanted to be with.

"So, I will write the body paragraphs and you write the introduction." I try to compromise on this project, but I would so much rather do this all by myself. I look at the school rented laptop in front of me, going through the outline of the paper.

"Blake, I can do more than just that." Logan grumbles, sitting all too close to me on his couch. For being brothers, they didn't look too much alike which I should be grateful for. I already struggle to focus on anything without thinking about Emmett.

"Logan, this is worth 25% of our grade, so in all honesty I would like to do it myself. You can do what I told you to do." I order, which I don't know where this new wave of confidence came from but I'm not upset.

"Yes, mommy, order me around more." Logan inches closer to me. "I usually like to be the one in charge, but I don't mind being a little submissive for you."

I jump off the couch at the sound of a knock at the door. It's stupid, but I have never even had a first kiss before. And I really didn't want Logan to hold the glory of that.

That's something special, the first kiss. The second or third, who even cares about that?

Emmett, he's the one who I would like to hold that glory. But I doubt he likes me like that.

"Yeah, dad, this is all the cash I have on me right now." Logan mutters at the door, blocking so I can't see the other figure.

He quickly closes the door, locking it. Not in

a creepy, he is going to murder me type of way, but more of a he doesn't want that guy who he called 'dad' to walk in.

"Can you not tell Emmett about this? Him and I are in the middle of a fight and this would not help." Logan sheepishly asks. Everyone in Chili's heard their little fight. It wasn't like Logan wasn't quiet or subtle about it.

"I really do have to go, I have work." I try to change the subject because I can't be like 'yeah, I won't tell Emmett when he picks me up from work tonight.' even though I want to.

I want to tell the man who asked me to be his 'mommy' that I would rather be with his hot older brother.

~~~~

"Did you actually get any of the project done with Logan?" Emmett asks as we sit parked behind my car, neither of us really wanting the night to end yet. My hair was up in a high ponytail and I could feel the headache coming along. I pull down my hair before it turns into a full blown headache, placing my hands awkwardly on my thighs.

I was in the weeds all night, I felt like I couldn't get ahead. It was the homecoming dance for one of the local high schools, so it was a ton of teenagers with seperate checks and no tips.

"Your brother, he umm" I try to think of what to tell him, I know he is asking to find out if his brother is okay. He didn't have to tell me, I knew from the first time I met them that Emmett was more like a father than a big brother. "It looked like he had eaten, at least from the dishes in his sink I could see that. He was doing okay, Emmett." I reassured him, it looked like a weight was lifted off his shoulders.

"Thank you." Emmett squeezes my hand that was placed on my thigh. I flip my hand over, letting him hold it. This is as bold as I can get with him. I still have that voice in the back of my head telling me that he would never like me. Which is easier to believe.

All I can focus on is the fact that he is holding my hand. We sit in silence, trying not to ruin the moment.

Maybe this is the furthest I will ever get with Emmett. Maybe we will never be anything more than friends, but the hope it will blossom into something more is still there.

CHAPTER 12
Emmett

I find myself counting down the time until I am outside waiting for Blake. Even as I'm under this car, changing the oil all I can think about is her. Which is why I don't remove the oil drain plug fast enough and I end up with oil all over my hands.

"God damn it." I push myself from under the car, I'm alone in the shop today. Mia is at my house still keeping an eye on Teddy, he can walk on his own now, but I don't think he should be alone just yet.

And Dean works more running the drug empire I have built than at the shop, he only brings people to me if they have fucked up or need some extra help.

That's how Mia got the job at the shop. Dean found her bloody and beaten after a client didn't pay her and her pimp took it out on her. He brought her to me to stitch up. I thought it was just that, but he begged me to give her a job in the shop and he would train her. Which meant we had to settle her debt with the pimp.

He would have paid anything to get Mia out of that place, but it isn't like he would ever admit that.

Dean acts like he doesn't care about the world, but he has always had a soft spot for Mia. So, I don't know how he's going to take the fact that she is now dating Teddy.

"Why the fuck are you outside of the Chili's that Blake works at every night?!" Logan comes storming towards me, anger radiating off of him. I don't even listen to the words he is saying, just looking him up and down making sure he is healthy. I look at his arms, trying to see if there are any warning signs that he is going down the same route as our mom.

"What?" I wipe my hands off on the nearest rag and toss it towards the laundry room. Laundry I need to do a load since Teddy hasn't been here and he is usually in charge of that, that was the last clean rag. Which means my jeans will be the next thing I will be using.

He shows me a snapchat story on his phone.

"Oh, Blake doesn't have to walk to her car because she has her man right outside." *The girl behind the phone says. Even in the poor lighting,*

Blake's beauty radiates off the screen.

"He's not my man." Blake giggles before she quickly hides away in my car.

"She is like a decade younger than you! No, more than a decade. That's fucking creepy. Stay away from my friends!" Logan continues to berate me.

"Blake is an adult, she can make her own decisions." I say.

"You have to have pressured her, I know you did. What did you threaten her with? You think I don't fucking know what you actually do for a living, I've known. You are no better than mom."

"Yeah, did your dad tell you about it? It's because he is one of our best customers." I bellowed. My fists forming, even if he considers me an old man I can still rock his shit. I always held back when we were younger and got into fist fights.

But if he wants me to treat him like an adult then he better be ready to fight like one as well.

"Fuck you, Emmett. She is never going to go for you. A high school dropout who's a drug dealer."

~~~~

"Boss, I found the ones who went after Teddy. Do you want me to deal with it?" Dean comes to the shop right after closing. It was a pretty uneventful day for me after Logan left.

"No. I want to deal with it." I angrily say. Logan got to me and I hate the feeling I have. I hate feeling like the monster he made me out to be.

"Emmett, I don't know what's going on with you and your brother. But I can handle this, you have a girl to go home to now." Dean is one of the few that I feel that I could confide in, but this was more than just the anger I was feeling towards Logan. I needed to show that no one messes with my people.

"Don't bring Blake into this." I growled, not realizing how I snapped at him when he didn't deserve it.

"You're not going alone. You are not in the right mind and I don't want you getting hurt."

I unlock my gun safe and put my glock 17 in the small of my back. This is probably the first time in a long time that I actually am nervous about something like this and I know it is because I actually have a person that I want to live for.

CHAPTER 13
Blake

No text messages, no calls, nothing. Emmett has fallen off the face of the earth once again. I should know better than to feel heartbroken about not seeing the black subie outside of the restaurant.

I was the last waitress to leave, so no one else got to see my disappointment.

I feel around in my bag for my pepper spray when the iconic black car shows up.

Yet, it's not Emmett in the driver's seat.

"Mia, right?" I ask the gorgeous girl from the shop. She looked serious, like this wasn't a social call. "W-where's Emmett?" My voice cracks.

"We gotta go." Mia answers. She speeds off before I even have a chance to put on my seatbelt. The thoughts are racing through my brain. Fuck, what do I tell my Grandma?

If I tell her the truth, she will never let me out of the house ever again. But if I don't say anything, that feels disrespectful.

I decided to text her that I am going to spend the night at a coworker's, so we can study together.

I know she won't question it too much, just that she's excited that I am making friends. But I do feel bad that I am lying to her.

"When this happened to Teddy, I wish I had someone who I could talk to." Mia breaks the silence, but I don't want to talk.

I know whatever Emmett and I have is new, but I can't lose him. I only really have my Grandma and Emmett in my life.

"You do know what he does for a living?" Mia glances over to me as I didn't answer her previous comment.

"I've heard the rumors." I mutter, picking at the skin around my nails out of anxiety.

"I didn't get a choice when it came to this life. You have a choice, so if you see him and it's too much, none of us are going to blame you if you want an out."

"Mia, I know we don't know each other very well. But I care about Emmett, so right now if he needs me then I will be there. We can deal with all of this bullshit later, but right now he needs me." I snap, tired of her looking down on me as a way to protect me.

I don't need protection.

The drive to his place was further than I expected, which made part of me guilty for the fact that he drives so far to come and see me every night. I'll definitely have a conversation with him about that later, but right now he needs me.

A pale and sweaty faced Emmett lays on his couch with a black cat on his pillow, trying to cuddle with him. He looked like death, but even in the midst of dying I am standing here in awe over him.

His face lit up the second he saw me, I didn't even care about the other person in the room. I ran to him with tears in my eyes.

"I'm sorry I didn't pick you up." His voice sounded deeper with how weak he was. He kisses the top of my head as I carefully hug him.

"Emmett Thornton, if you ever scare me like this again I will be the one needing help with hiding your body." I jokingly say, pulling back now able to fully see his wounds. The bloody gauze bundled up on his shoulder is what catches my eye.

"That's where I come in. Dean." A light brown hair man with green eyes, who looked no older than me emerges with more gauze and meds for Emmett. "Em, you gotta take something for the pain."

"No pain killers." Emmett grits through his teeth, holding my hand tightly as Dean stitches up his shoulder. I should turn away and gag, but instead I'm watching Dean stitch him up. With each tug of the skin and knot, I start to think about all those medical shows I used to watch.

And it's not like the movies.

Maybe it is because we are doing it on a couch and not in a hospital, but still.

"You should take something." I whisper, kissing his hand.

"I took some ibuprofen." He groans in pain, squeezing my hand. Dean slaps the wound after bandaging it up. "Fuck you, Dean."

"You wish I would let you." Dean chuckles, taking the dirty gauze to the trash before Emmett could muster up enough energy to attack him back.

Emmett painfully moved on the couch making room for me to lay next to him as his good shoulder was closer to the inside of the couch, he pulled me into the spot.

I feel too big to be on the couch with him, I've never been a small girl with my curves and boobs, so I feel insecure in moments like this. But he doesn't say anything, just holding me with my head on his good shoulder.

The cat that was once on top of the couch, is trying to snuggle with me and Emmett.

"You're the hurt one, shouldn't I be taking care of you?" I trace my fingers over the tattoos on his chest, there are two tigers one on each pec. One is covered up with the gauze, but I wonder if they are supposed to be him and Logan.

Should I call Logan? No, that's not my business. But maybe I should.

"This is better than any pain meds out there." His voice was low. I made the decision, he isn't drugged up so he is in the right state of mind and I almost lost him. I'm done waiting for him to make the first move.

I look up, grabbing his face and kissing him. It's my goddamn first kiss and I will have it with who I want.

I wait for him to pull back as I must have read the situation wrong or something, but he doesn't. He wraps his good arm around me and pulls me closer to him, kissing me harder.

Now that is a first kiss for the books.

CHAPTER 14
Blake

I couldn't sleep, I kept on waking up to make sure he was still breathing. It was a mission in itself to get out of Emmett's grasp, so I could make myself busy and make breakfast.

With Dean asleep in one bed and Teddy and Mia asleep in another, this is a full house and I felt like I was going crazy since time could not go any slower.

Emmett has a pretty stocked kitchen, so the hard part was deciding what to make.

"Is that french toast I smell?" Groggily Emmett slowly walks into the kitchen.

"You should not be walking around by yourself! I could have helped you!" I scold, throwing the spatula

on the counter to help him to the barstools at the island.

"I didn't know if I was dreaming when it came to that kiss, so I wanted to investigate myself.

Worst case it was Dean that I kissed, best case it was you." He adjusts the sling that his left arm was in, still shirtless. The butterflies and the tingles on my lips were still there from the kiss. I slide him a plate with french toast, bacon, and eggs.

"Coffee?" I hold up the pot of coffee, trying not to stare at him for too long. I'm still nervous and giddy around him, even if last night I had the ability to take control.

"Blake, come over here before I get up and you yell at me again." Emmett holds his arm out. Once I get within arms reach, he pulls me in closing the distance.

His lips finding mine, the taste of syrup and butter is still lingering on his lips.

"Do we have to kiss the chef to get breakfast?" Dean interrupts us and I pull away. At this moment, I hate that I am still in my uniform from work and how uncomfortable I am. Maybe it is the embarrassment of being caught that is making me overthink it.

"You even think about doing that and I will use my good arm to murder you." Emmett threatens his friend, holding my waist tighter.

"Ooo, like I am scared of a man with one good shoulder who can barely walk." Dean mocks as he takes a piece of bacon from Emmett's plate.

I pull myself out of Emmett's arms, so I can pull the food out of the oven where I had it hidden so it would stay warm. I quietly made the other boy a plate while the two of them talked as if I wasn't here.

"Have you told Logan?" Dean inquires after thanking me for the plate.

"He doesn't want to know." Emmett angrily grumbles.

"Breakfast?! I fucking like this one, Emmett. She is way better than the other girls you would bring around." Teddy jokes as he strolls into the kitchen with Mia.

Other girls?

I mean look at him, I couldn't expect that he spent the last 32 years waiting for me to show up. But is it wrong that I kind of hoped that's how it would be?

CHAPTER 15

Emmett

Why did Teddy have to say that? Blake didn't have to say anything for me to know that she was uncomfortable about that false statement. I'm not some womanizer.

Like god, the only way I was able to get a woman in the last 10 years is by getting shot in the shoulder. And she had to make the first fucking move.

Mia hits Teddy before I could, which is probably good. I want to pretend like I feel better because I don't want Blake to worry about me, but I don't.

Dean really dug around to get the bullet out of my shoulder, not caring about the pain I was in. I wouldn't expect him to, he needed to do what he needed to do.

And my refusal of taking pain meds isn't helping.

"Teddy is an ass, don't listen to him." Dean

informs Blake. "I kind of thought that Emmett was some kind of weird drug dealing priest."

"I'm so close to kicking all of you out of my fucking house." I mutter, standing up to go to my room, so I could change. Everyone reached for me as I got up too quickly and was a little wobbly. "I'm fine. I've gotten shot in much worse places."

"Yeah, but that was when you were young. Now you are an old man." Teddy reminds me.

"Where are you wanting to go?" Blake whispers to me, holding out her hand. Now that's a hand I will hold.

"Just upstairs and to the left." I say. Blake quietly leads me to my room, making sure I am not about to pass out from pain.

"I want you to know that they are all stupid." I tell Blake, sitting on my bed. She insisted that I had to sit on the bed while she found my clothes and I was not about to argue with her.

"Oh, it's okay." She quietly says, but I know that is more than that. I can tell by the way she is acting.

"No, Blake I want you to know, it is kind of embarrassing but there hasn't been another girl. There hasn't been a girl in a long while." I don't want to tell her the exact amount of time because that is even more embarrassing.

"So, you really are a drug dealing priest?" Blake giggles, handing me a pair of gray sweatpants and black boxer briefs. I can't really wear a shirt right now, so this is my full outfit.

"I wanted to explain that part to you. I didn't want you to find out this way." I didn't have a plan on how to tell her about this. It isn't like there is a Wiki page on how to tell a girl you like that you are a drug dealer.

"You don't have to explain yourself. Here I will give you some privacy so you can change."

I reach out for her, stopping her from leaving. I didn't realize how much I longed for human touch, but after last night I was craving for more of her. "I do need to explain myself. Look, I didn't have a great childhood, so I did the things I did to keep food on the table for Logan and get him through college. I told myself once he graduated, I would stop and go back and get my GED. He doesn't want my help anymore, so I actually could."

"It really is okay." Blake answers.

"Blake, I am not going to hold you hostage here, so if this is too much for you I can get Mia to drive you back." I sigh, knowing that this was the reality of my life.

"Emmett, yeah this is a lot for me, but maybe I am crazy." Blake stops her sentence and stands on her tippy toes to kiss me. I wish I wasn't injured, so I could lift her to toss her on my bed. The things I want to do to her.

But maybe this injury is a sign that I should take things slow with her.

CHAPTER 16
Blake

I don't want to overstay my welcome. I've been here for 2 days and Emmett doesn't seem like he's complaining. He actually is enjoying my company and all the food I've been making him.

He gave me some of his clothes to wear and with my curves, they fit a lot tighter than it would have fit most.

"My doctor said I could shower today." Emmett looks at his cellphone and then back up at me as I was feeding Crucio. He explained to me that Crucio hates almost everyone, except him and I. So, he was beyond happy to see his cat and I conversing and cuddling one afternoon.

"You mean Dean?" I giggle, he wraps his good arm around my waist.

"I mean, me. I'm saying I could shower today, but I think I need some help." His hot breath against my ear, he kisses down my neck to my shoulder.

"Emmett," I quietly moan. "I need to tell you something..." I whisper, snapping back to reality. I want to shower with him, but I have never seen a naked man in person before. I've never been naked in front of someone like this before. There are so many thoughts rushing through my mind.

"Yes, little lady?" He murmurs against my neck.

"You're my first. First kiss, everything." I quickly say. "So,"

"God, I can't wait to corrupt you." Emmett cuts me off, not letting me give him an 'out'. Instead he drags me to the bathroom.

If he wasn't injured, I would have expected him to throw me over his shoulder with how quickly he was dragging me to the bathroom.

I help Emmett with his shirt and sling, running my fingers over his tattoos, carefully tracing them.

"I hate that I'm fucking injured. The things I want to do to you." He tugs at the bottom of my shirt, telling me to take it off. I stopped wearing a bra after the first 24 hours of being his caretaker. I could only wear the same bra for a day or two before I had to switch it out. "You are so beautiful," He whispers, admiring my breasts.

"So, are you." I can't take my eyes off of him,

blood rushing to his cheeks from the compliment. I gotta make him blush more often because it legit made my heart skip a beat.

I kick off the pair of boxer briefs that I borrowed from him, Emmett follows my lead. He pushes me into the shower, closing the glass door behind us.

"I'm so goddamn selfish, all I want to do is keep you here forever." Emmett pushes me against the shower wall, knocking down the bottles of soap. Our laughter filled the room. Is it possible to find someone's laugh attractive? Because his laugh is something I could listen to on repeat for the rest of my life.

"I think we would have to tell my Grandma something sooner or later before she goes all Liam Neeson on you." I joke.

"I run a drug empire, I think I could take your Grandma."

"Says the one with a bullet in his shoulder."

Our bubble is popped as the sound of a male's voice is being shouted through the house. Emmett shoves me behind him, opening the glass door and grabbing a gun that was hidden.

He holds a finger to his mouth telling me to be quiet.

"Emmett Grayson Thornton!" The voice becomes louder and more familiar. Logan.

The bathroom door is thrown open and a disheveled Logan in one of his many frat shirts and shorts. He looks hungover and a mess.

"Either shoot me or put the gun away. Why do I have to find out from my fucking father that you were shot?! You have been so busy playing house with Blake that you didn't think of fucking telling me? I'm your brother!" Logan yells, not caring that Emmett and I are both naked.

"Logan, you don't get to just come into my house and lecture me because you heard something from your drug addict daddy." Emmett puts the gun back in its hiding space. "Now you're letting all the heat out."

"You fucking bastard. So, your life is too dangerous for me to be a part of, but you can let Blake be a part of it? I guess I know which part you think with."

"My life is too fucking dangerous for you to be a part of. You want to know how I got this injury? I killed some men who jumped one of the people I care about. I kill people who mess with the people I care about. Which is why I keep you far away from this because I have pissed off many people in my life trying to keep food on the table. And they will use you to hurt me. Now stop fucking checking out *my girl,* and get out of here." Emmett slams the glass door shut, I worried that it was going to shatter from how angry he was. I stand frozen in the corner of the shower.

This man has so many red flags, that I should run the other way. But what should I say? I love the color red.

CHAPTER 17
Emmett

Blake and I didn't speak after Logan left. We finished showering with me handing her soap even though I would have rather have helped her.

But I didn't want to push it.

"You probably have some questions." I broke the silence with an obvious statement after we both dressed. Blake helped me with my shirt, even if I didn't ask her. "Ask away."

"Why?" Blake quietly asks, sitting on my bed criss-cross applesauce.

"Why what?"

"Why do any of this?" She asks a little louder.

I made the decision to drop out long before I came to this decision. It was easy to drop out, forging my mom's signature is something I learned how to do before I knew how to sign my own name.

"Emmett, what can I do for you?" Charlie, one of my mom's friends asks as he smokes a cigarette by

69

his car. I knew the bar he would frequent, so it was easy to find him.

For being one of my mom's friends, he always had the nicest things. His car always looked out of place at our trailer.

"Give me a job." I demanded, I thought about how I was going to ask this for days. But I went with a statement over asking.

"Finish school, get a degree and go get a job in the real world. You don't want to be a part of my world." Charlie takes a long drag of his cigarette. His reddish brown hair always looks more red in the sunlight. As a child, I always called him Chucky because his hair had a slight red tint to it. And probably because he made me watch it as a 5 year old.

"That isn't an option. I don't know if you noticed but Logan hasn't grown in the last year because he isn't eating. He starts kindergarten in the fall, I can't have CPS called on us again. They will separate us and he won't last a minute in a group home. And I don't know if you noticed, but mom only comes home when our food stamps show up. Either you give me a job or I will go find someone else."

Charlie wraps his hand around my throat, pushing me to the ground. "You never fucking give me an ultimatum. That's not how this works. If you want a job, you have to climb the fucking ladder like everyone else. You will do what is asked of you and you will not have any of those smart ass remarks. Now pick yourself off the ground, you look pathetic. Let's go."

"For Logan. I spent my childhood in and out of group homes, foster homes, you name it I was there. I was slipping birth control in my mom's food long before I knew how to write my own name, but then she stopped coming home. And next thing I know we are preparing for a new baby brother. She was always the best when she was pregnant or breastfeeding, clean. But once Logan was no longer breastfeeding, it fell on me to feed him. It got real bad after she had a miscarriage a couple years after Logan. I rarely saw her and stealing was not enough. I wasn't old enough for a real job and he was so small. Which is hard to believe when you see him now, but he wouldn't cry from hunger pains because he didn't have enough energy to do that." I stare down at my hand that's stuck in the sling, unable to look Blake in the eyes as I admit this. "The bank was threatening to foreclose on our trailer. I couldn't go back to the streets, not with Logan. That's how CPS would get called and they would have separated us. People don't want a teenager, so I would have been sent to a group home until I aged out. If we were lucky, Logan would have been sent to a good family to never know who I was. But worst case, he would age out of a group home with nothing to his name."

"So, what are you? A serial killer? But with morals?" Blake asks.

"No, I don't seek people out and kill them. It's not like that."

"Then what is it, Emmett?" Her voice cracking, this is a lot for someone to take in. I understand that.

"I protect the ones I care about."

CHAPTER 18
Blake

His eyes darkened with the statement, looking up from his hands.

"I brought you into this life and I will be damned if something happens to you." Emmett growled. "You don't understand the things I would do to someone if they even thought about hurting you."

"Says the man with one arm." I joke because that's what I do, I try to make light of scary situations.

"I can do more with one arm than most can do with two."

~~~~

"Emmett, I do have to go back to work." I say with his arm wrapped around me. "And this crazy thing called school."

"Can I just pay for you to stay?" Emmett sleepily asks, not opening his eyes.

"I'm not a hooker, so no."

"Wait, you're not my 10 o'clock?!" Emmett smiles, opening his eyes. "You're not the red headed hooker I requested. But I guess you'll do." He kisses me, not caring about the fact that I probably have bad morning breath.

"So, you have a type? Do you seek out red heads?" I raise an eyebrow.

"Do you seek out drug dealing mechanics?" He teases right back, knowing damn well that he's my first for everything.

"Yeah, I put an ad on Craigslist. Many interviewed, but I settled for you. In all seriousness I really gotta go to my classes sooner or later. You're the one who's so pro-education."

"I mean I guess you're right. Teddy dropped your car off last night. Your keys are on the hook by the door." Emmett admits defeat in trying to keep me here. I wouldn't mind that. The couple days have been the happiest I've been in a while.

I wouldn't let myself feel happy after my parents died, the guilt of being responsible for it.

But I haven't felt that guilt while with Emmett, it is like nothing matters when I'm with him.

CHAPTER 19

Emmett

Logan hasn't spoken to me since he caught Blake and I in the shower together. I have reached out to him multiple times and he won't answer. My reaction wasn't the best, but I was naked and had a beautiful girl in the shower with me.

I had plans that he interrupted. I wasn't thinking with my brain at that specific moment.

I want to have my brother back.

"God damnit." I mutter slamming my phone down. I'm tired of being injured, I'm tired of Logan being an ass. It's selfish that at this moment I am thinking back to the mornings spent with Blake in my bed and not the fact that my brother has sent my call to voicemail once again.

"Boss, your girl is out front." Teddy sticks his head in my office. I got him a new hat, like his hurt self had complained out. Even though I'm not a baseball fan, he loves the black Giants hat that he constantly wears.

Even though I can barely do any work, I still wore my coveralls. I guess it makes me feel like I have a purpose by coming to the shop.

"Little lady, what do I owe this pleasure?" I immediately feel the weight lifted off my shoulder, the second I see her red hair in the distance.

"My Grandma insisted that I would bring my 'friend' with the shoulder injury some cupcakes. You know because all doctors recommend for a bullet wound, is sugar." She smiles, holding a plate of chocolate cupcakes with a light brown frosting.

"From my extensive medical knowledge I would say that this is exactly what the doctor ordered." I put the plate on top of the tool cabinet against the wall, using my good arm to pull her closer to me. Kissing her, the taste of coffee still lingering on her lips.

"As your doctor I would say that I do accept payment in chocolate… what kind of frosting is that?" Dean looks over the plate. He has come in to pick up what I haven't been able to do. With only Mia working, we would have been so behind and that's not fair. These people are paying good money for our work.

"Peanut butter." Blake giggles against my lips.

"Stay away from my cupcakes, man!" I yell,

snapping my head around as the three of them are already diving into them.

"I have more at home." Blake whispers. "But I gotta go to work. I just wanted to make sure you weren't overworking yourself."

"You want to come by after work?" I ask, hoping that she says yes. I was going to walk her to her car with Teddy around the corner to take me home. Nobody trusts me to experiment with driving with one working shoulder.

"I would love to."

~~~~

Despite the yells, I told them to all go to hell and let me work on something. I didn't care about the pain in my shoulder, I could work through it.

I wasn't meant to be behind a desk.

"6 hours. Who had 6 hours?" Teddy yells out, waving cash in the air.

"That was Mia." Dean reads off his phone. "In under 8 hours."

"You guys were taking bets on me?" I pushed myself from under the car, I was doing an oil change. I can do those in my sleep, so one armed is nothing.

"Oh, we have a ton of bets on you. Dean won

for how long it took you to get laid." Teddy informs me.

"10 years and 8 months. It only took Blake coming into your life." Dean proudly admits.

"Blake and I haven't had sex. Not that I want to discuss my sex life with my employees, but Dean needs to give the money back." I wipe my hands off on a rag, trying carefully to not move my shoulder too much. I can work through most of this pain, but Blake really lectured me about giving my body time to heal.

I told her it would be a lot easier to give my body time to heal if she was in the bed next to me. However, she had to go to school and stuff and I can't stay locked in my house. I will go crazy.

"Is this really what you guys are doing with the drug empire that *I* built? That you stole from me?" The familiar dark voice says. I don't even give it a second thought before pulling my gun out of the tool box that was next to me.

The clicking sound behind me indicates that the other three had the same plan as me. They have my back and that's all I can ask for in a team.

"*Charlie,*" I seethed, ready to kill the man in front of me. The stray gray strands blend into his hair and the facial hair he never once sported now lays prominent on his face. He may have aged, but

I still recognize him.

"I just want you to know that I've been keeping tabs on you. Blake is an excellent waitress. It would be a shame," Charlie holds his hands up to show that he is unarmed, but inches closer to me.

"You even think about hurting her." I threaten, ready to kill him and get this over with. But it is still light out and far too many people would report the sound of a gun going off. This isn't the place.

Dean is the one who usually cleans up the bodies and he's damn good at hiding them. But this would be one mess he wouldn't be able to hide.

"You pissed a lot of people off when you double crossed me. Logan was easy. Getting his father to beg him for money, knowing that sweet old Logan would do it. Thus getting Logan out from under your thumb, but Blake. She's been harder. Or maybe her sweet old Grandma? Heard that's all she has left in her life." Charlie says. This man would kick me while I was down, literally and figuratively. It made me stronger, strong enough to take his throne.

I say fuck it to my gun, wrapping my hand around his throat, pushing him against the car. I watch as the more pressure I put, the more he begins to struggle. I don't want to kill him right now, but I want him to know that I could if I tried.

"Threaten me all you want, but fucking stay away from Blake and Logan. Remember I know all of your moves, you taught me them." I throw him to the ground, the pain of my wound being opened back up is background noise as all I can think about is Blake and her safety.

Charlie coughing on the ground, holding his throat in pain.

"I told you before, a girl makes you soft. You are going to regret not pulling that trigger." Charlie scrambles away.

Maybe I should have pulled that trigger. Dean has cleaned up worse, but something stopped me.

I just can't let Blake out of my sight.

CHAPTER 20

Blake

"Who won the bet?" I spot the grease that Emmett missed on his hand that he was hiding in his sling.

"You even knew about the bet??" He asks in shock, taking my backpack from me to carry it.

"Teddy asked if I wanted to join in. But the minimum buy-in was too much." I admit, interlacing my fingers with his.

I'm selfish because when Emmett was telling me that he wouldn't be able to drive since he doesn't own an automatic car, I was sad that he wouldn't be waiting for me after work.

"Fuck. Should I ask what the buy-in was?" Emmett seems off, like he keeps on checking out surroundings as we walk. It could be because we are walking and not driving to my car, but he holds me real close to him.

"You really shouldn't." I laugh handing the keys over to him. I was far too tired to do the

40 minute drive to his house and I still have homework to do.

The first part of our group project is due this weekend and I haven't talked to Logan about it since he saw me in the shower with his brother.

"I know it's a waste because we will literally drive right by it. But I really don't want to wait in a drive thru line. Can we order McDonald's on DoorDash?" I ask, taking my spot as passenger princess. Teddy has been calling me that nonstop since they found out about me and what Emmett has been driving so much just to see me for a couple minutes.

"Of course, little lady." Emmett chuckles, turning on my car. It takes him a minute to figure out how he's going to shift gears, but he quickly does it. "When did this check engine light come on?"

"Oh, that light. So after you fixed it, the light was gone, but it turned back on like a week ago." I scroll through the McDonald's page on Doordash as if I haven't been thinking about this my whole shift. "Do you want to split some chicken nuggets with me? I could order a four pack, but I want 5 chicken nuggets. And 6 seems like too much. So, then 10 is out of the question. Because I am getting a big mac meal and I don't want a chicken nugget meal." I don't even realize that I am rambling until

Emmett begins to chuckle. "Shit, I really don't know how to be around a man. Like should I be acting like I only eat salads, which isn't a bad thing, but it isn't me?"

"Little lady, never feel bad about what you want to eat and anyone who makes you feel that way can deal with me. And yes, I will share nuggets with you." Emmett instinctively goes to hold my thigh as he drives, but quickly grabs the wheel. "I hate this fucking sling."

He throws the sling off, wincing in pain.

"Do I want to know how you hurt yourself more?" I ask, looking over my screen.

"Just make sure to order me a McChicken." Emmett changes the subject, putting his right hand on my thigh. Even with his large hands, they can't cover all of my thighs. But that doesn't stop him from trying to hold all of my thick thighs. "Much better. And you are leaving this car at my shop, so I can figure out what's wrong."

~~~~

"Why are you in my house?" Emmett asks Dean, Teddy, and Mia while he is holding the bags of takeout. Crucio immediately comes up to Emmett and I, doing loops around our legs making sure to rub himself against it.

"You have better alcohol." Dean answers

from the bar cart, pouring himself another drink. "You want one, Blake?"

"No thank you." I mutter, really only caring about the food that I ordered. Emmett wouldn't let me pay for food as he said it is his turn after I made him so much food while he was healing.

"Can you give her a moment? She has been working since 5 am between both of her jobs and school. Neither of us expected for there to be company." Emmett scolded them, which makes me feel guilty. I don't want to be a damper to their party, but it does feel good to have someone stand up for me.

It feels good to not be alone and against the world and to have someone on my side.

After showering, changing into some of Emmett's clothes, and eating, I do feel ready to face the party downstairs. Emmett and I ate in his bed with the TV as loud as we could, so we could feel like we still got to have dinner together.

"So, do you want a drink now, Blake?" Teddy now asks me as I walk down the stairs, his arm wrapped around Mia.

Mia hasn't said much to me since the day she picked me up. It felt like a vulnerable moment for her, something that is rare.

"Yeah, I have hard liquor over there or

beer and other drinks like that in the fridge in the garage." Emmett kisses the top of my head, wrapping his arm around my waist. "You look so good in my clothes. I should let you wear them more often." He whispers in my ear, making me giggle as the butterflies intensify in my stomach. His black hair is wet from the shower that he wouldn't let me take by myself. Not that I'm complaining.

"I've never drank before." I whisper, hoping that only Emmett would hear me.

"Oh fuck yeah, she has to try everything." Teddy shoots up from the couch running to the garage.

Good thing I finished all my homework that's due tonight.

CHAPTER 21

Blake

"Okay, so that's vodka, then tequila, then gin. Just take them back to back." Teddy lines up three shots for me. "So, you can take the shot and chase it with whatever you are drinking there."

"Were you a fan of what you had for dinner?" Dean comes behind me to ask.

"Why?" I look at him suspiciously, holding the first shot glass in my hand with a seagrams in my other.

"Because you are never going to want to eat that again after tonight." Dean warns. Emmett crosses the room to see what kind of bullshit his friends are roping me into.

"She is not taking three shots back to back. Are you trying to give her alcohol poisoning?" Emmett scolds them, he was drinking a beer in a glass bottle. I don't know what the brand was, but he had me try a sip and it was so gross.

"That was the goal." Dean smirks and

Emmett attacks him with his one good arm. "Old man I can beat your ass even without your hurt shoulder. Speaking of being an old man, how old are you Blake?" Dean asks, using me as a shield from Emmett.

"20." I place the shot back down, actually a little nervous to take it. They don't look enjoyable to take.

"Damn, well we should tell you we do not condone underage drinking." Emmett jokes.

"So, you will sell me drugs but not alcohol?" I ask.

"Exactly."

~~~~

"Alcohol tastes like shit, but this is so much fun! Why didn't I go to parties and shit in high school and do this?" I loudly yell even though there is no music or anything that I would have to speak over. My whole head felt fuzzy, but I felt good. I wasn't stressed about school or work, I was just enjoying the moment with them.

"Take another one!" Teddy hands me another shot. It has gotten easier to take them as the night has grown, but this one almost came up. Don't worry I am not a spitter, so I got it back down.

"Little lady, you should slow down." Emmett pulls me onto his lap.

"When are you going to fuck me?" I bluntly ask, making him choke on his drink. "Like I had to make the first move to kiss you, but I have slept in your bed almost every night for the last week and you haven't made a single move. I've seen your cock, you don't have anything to be shy about."

"Yes, go on Blake. What else about Emmett can you tell us?" Dean chuckles at Emmett's embarrassment. "You know he's basically a virgin, so you can't blame him."

"How can you be 'basically a virgin'?" I look at Emmett innocently and back at Dean, knowing that Emmett will probably not answer this.

"After being celibate for 10 years, you get your virginity back." Teddy answers.

"Damn Teddy, you actually know what the word celibate means? I'm glad to see your word a day calendar has worked out." I insult Teddy without even thinking about it. I would never act like this if it wasn't for the alcohol. Mia sits next to Teddy, not partaking in the conversation or the drinking. Maybe she is the designated driver.

"Little lady, I haven't fucked you because I don't want to. I think you and I both *know* I have been more than excited to be around you. I want to be able to fuck you when I am physically healthy. I want to make your first time memorable." Emmett whispers in my ear, kissing my neck. His erection pressing against my butt.

"Here, take this shot." Teddy hands me another shot which I take without question.

"She is like one shot away from puking all over you guys." Emmett hands me a glass of water to drink, but the water is harder to drink than the shot.

"That's the plan." Teddy is pouring another shot which Emmett puts a stop to.

"I don't feel so good." I burp, holding onto Emmett as the world starts to move too quickly. It needs to slow down if I am quite honest. It's crazy how quickly it went from fun to pain.

"Well, you guys emptied my liquor cabinet so get out of my house before I have to kill you all for being a bad influence on my girl." Emmett stands up, holding onto me tightly. Even with his injured shoulder, he is still so strong. He carries me up the stairs, placing me gently on the ground next to the toilet. I hold my arm up, so he can grab my hair tie off my wrist.

He takes the hint, messily putting my hair up.

"God, alcohol is the worst." I hiccup, placing

my face against the cold toilet bowl.

"I know, little lady." He kisses my forehead.

"I have to go to Logan's tomorrow to work on my project. What am I supposed to say after he saw me naked in the shower with his brother?" I cry, the guilty feelings all coming back to me from that day.

"If he wants to talk about it, then he can talk to me about it. You are there to work on school work not to discuss your sex life."

"Or my lack of."

"Little lady, you will regret saying that you lack a sex life soon enough." He hints, rubbing my back slowly.

CHAPTER 22

Emmett

I need to see my mom. I have my reasons for not visiting her, but Logan and I have never gone this long without contact. It is time to tattle.

Just because I don't speak to my mom doesn't mean that I don't take care of her. I bought out her lot in the trailer park long ago and her new husband takes care of the other bills now.

He isn't my biggest fan. Probably has to do with the fact that I am the biggest contributor to our drug problem in this town and he is a pastor who encourages youth to stay away from me.

Yeah, she married a pastor.

The familiar front door that used to be barely hanging on the hinges, but I replaced it after her first time in rehab. That's where she met her husband.

He would come every Sunday, so that the patients could attend service if they wanted to. My very atheist mother saw him as a way to get drugs while on the inside.

I don't know when the relationship changed nor do I care.

"Mom?" I yell out after letting myself in, the smell of chocolate chip cookies filling the air. She never baked for us, well it is hard to bake for children that you never see.

"Emmett?" She pokes her head out of the kitchen, the grays in her hair showing more than I remember. My mom and Logan could be twins, whereas I was the black sheep. Quite literally.

"I know Adam won't like that I'm here. I promise I will be out of here before the kids are off the bus." I look up at the clock, Blake is going to be out of class soon, so if I time this correctly I can meet her with some coffee before her next class.

"Honey, what's wrong with your arm?" My mom immediately clocks how I am favoring my right arm far more than my left. Even though I can work through the pain and I'm going to keep on pushing myself I subconsciously do shit like this.

"Consequences of the job, but I'm not here to talk about that. Have you heard anything from Logan? He has gone radio silence with me." I ask, not taking the seat my mom has offered me.

"He came over on Saturday like he usually does to hang with your brothers."

"Step brothers." I correct her because Adam makes sure I know that. Logan is allowed to be a part of this family because he is going to college and is worthy of a family in their eyes.

But I am not.

"He seemed fine. He did mention that you are seeing a girl who is much younger than you and how gross that was. But he doesn't understand how great it is that you are finally allowing yourself to be happy."

"I'm not here to talk about Blake."

"Blake Sanders? No, no, no. You have to stay away from her." My mom almost drops the dish in her hand when I said Blake's name. Oh, I *should* stay away from someone. I think she should be staying away from me.

"Just because her mom and you had some fall out does not mean that you get to decide who I date." I annoyingly say as Blake had mentioned in passing that our mothers knew each other. They grew up in the same neighborhood, but the age difference was significant enough that I didn't think much about it.

"You were too young to remember, but she would babysit you. Charlie was in love with her, or maybe it was lust. I never knew, but then she graduated and ran off with some other guy. Charlie was never the same, but I know that red hair anywhere. I will tell you this one more time, stay away from Blake." My mom orders like she has the right to parent me.

"I know I still call you, mom, but you lost the chance to parent me decades ago. It is too late to do so. Tell Logan to stop avoiding me." I walk out of the house, not turning my back to see her face. There is only one woman in my life that matters to me. And it isn't the one who I left speechless in her kitchen.

The coffee shop on campus wasn't as crowded as I expected it to be. I wish I could be one of these students. My plan was always to go to Harvard, I had my eyes set on that.

I wanted to get as far away from this town as possible.

But that doesn't mean I regret the life I chose.

I was smart with my money, protecting myself from more than just people like Charlie. Money is powerful, so when you own most of the town people will turn a blind eye to the fact that I am supplying this town with every drug possible.

So, maybe I don't have a fancy degree on my wall. But I have something so much better. Power.

At the end of the day, these choices led me to

the redheaded beauty that is walking towards me. Her jeans hugged her curves, making me wonder how I got so lucky to have her in my life.

The weather had dropped in the last couple days adding a chill to the air, so I should not be surprised that she stole my sweatshirt that has my mechanic shop logo on it.

I feel a sense of pride knowing that as boys check her out, they see my last name on her left breast.

"A filthy chai?" I hold out the warm drink in front of me. Blake said in passing that she loves her chai to be as she said 'a dirty fucking slut' in regards to how many shots of espresso in it.

"You are a godsend. I have a three hour lecture next and I was debating on throwing myself in front of a car to get out of it." She brings the drink to her lips, taking a long sip of it.

"I think I clawed my way from hell. I don't think God had anything to do with me."

CHAPTER 23

Blake

I hide the sweatshirt in the bottom of my backpack, so that my grandma doesn't see the name 'Thornton's mechanic shop' across my left boob. I haven't seen her in almost a week, so I don't need that to be the first thing she sees.

I think she is just happy that I am not hiding out in my room anymore, so she doesn't mind that I haven't been home in over a week.

I also don't want to overstay my welcome. I only ever stay when Emmett asks me to.

"You're alive! So, who is this boy?" My grandma rises from the recliner. The warm open arms of my grandma gives me the kind of comfort that I need.

"Grandma, there isn't much to say about him." I actually have so much to say about Emmett. But I can't say those things to the one who told me to stay away from him.

"Okay, tell me how you two met?" She

continues to try to pry.

"Through his brother. He's kind of older than me. Like 12 years..." I mumble the last part.

"All that means is he has money to spoil you, which is all that matters. You're an adult, so who cares. Grandpa was ten years older than me. And older men know what they want in bed."

"Grandma, I really don't want to discuss my sex life with you. I feel like that's a little too weird." I start to head down the hall to my bedroom, so I can grab what I need to go back to Emmett's after I work. He doesn't like that I am still working my two jobs, as he hates how tired I am all the time. But I refuse to take his money, so this is what I have to do.

"Just use protection! I'm too young to be a great grandma!" She yells at me.

~~~~

"Are you sure I'm not bothering you?" I sit in the corner of his garage as he works out, Crucio lays in my lap.

"Little lady, you are never bothering me. And I should probably have someone out here because of my shoulder. And you are far more fun to look at than Teddy or Dean." Emmett racks the bar on the squat rack, hanging over it. His hair was falling in his face from the sweat, he used his shirt to wipe the sweat away from his face.

"I just know I have spent a lot of time here. I don't want you to get tired of me. I don't even know what *this* is." I look down at Crucio, the cat who never wants to be around anyone yet he is sitting in my lap.

"You're my little lady. You're mine." Emmett abandons his workout picking me off the ground.

"Your shoulder, Em." I squeal as I wrap my legs around him.

"It's easy to ignore the pain when I have you to focus on. I want to show you how much I enjoy your presence."

Emmett lays me down on his bed, kissing my neck. Have his kisses always felt this good? Something about his kisses feel electrifying right now. I can feel them through my whole body, sending shivers.

"God, you are so beautiful." He mutters against my skin. He hasn't even touched me that way, yet everything feels so electrifying. His finger trails at the end of my shirt. I reach down and pull it off for him, so he doesn't have to have that internal debate anymore. "I love your boobs. That first time you agreed to shower with me, I almost came right then and there. I had plans for that shower. But of course…"

He kisses each of my nipples, biting them softly making a moan escape my lips. I'm so used to quietly masturbating in my room that I didn't even think I knew how to make those noises I hear in porn.

"But tonight, I'm taking my time. I've been waiting for this for 10 goddamn years and I will be savoring you." Emmett rips off my pants along with my underwear.

"I know you have seen me naked, but I should have shaved or something. They are always shaved in the porn videos I've seen." I feel the blood rushing to my face from embarrassment.

"What I would pay to watch you watch porn and masturbate. God, little lady. I don't care if you shave or don't shave, all I have been thinking about since I first saw you was getting between your legs." He shuts me up, lowering his head and kissing my thick thighs.

His hot breath ghosted over the spot that I wanted him the most, bucking my hips. "E-Emmett," I quietly beg.

"Patience, little lady. I said I am savoring this." His hands grip my hips, holding me in place. His nails digging into my skin, bringing me more pleasure. "Relax and let me pleasure you."

"How am I supposed to relax?" I stammer,

still embarrassed by how intimate this is. Emmett looks up from between my legs with a warm smile.

All my insecure thoughts were pushed aside by pleasure with his finger slowly pumping, I *need* more.

"That's it, little lady. I know what I'm doing and let me do this for you." His tongue dips between my folds. I grip the bed sheets, arching my back off the bed. "You taste so good." He mumbles against my pussy. Emmett removes his fingers and before I can complain about the loss of it, he grips my ass pulling me closer to his mouth.

One of my hands trails over my body, grabbing ahold of my breast and massaging it. My eyes begin to flutter closed from pleasure.

Emmett stops making my eyes shoot back open.

"I want you to watch me, I want your eyes on me until you cum or else I will stop. Understand?" His voice deepens as he barks the orders at me. I simply nod, locking eyes with his dark blue eyes. His eyes filled with lust and desire, deepening the color.

His fingers returned, pumping faster. My thighs tighten around his head as the feeling builds. He rewards me with a low groan sending vibrations against my clit.

My legs begin to shake, but he doesn't stop his rhythm. Emmett steadily continues to guide me to the end of my orgasm, my moans encouraging him. He is a fucking god.

Once back on earth, he is released from my grasp which he brings his fingers to my lips. Having me taste the pleasure he brought to me.

Emmett's phone begins to ring, which I just hope he would ignore. But it is late and no one would call him this late unless it was important.

"This better be important. Someone better be dead or else someone will be, for interrupting me." Emmett angrily says into his phone. I know he is serious about the second part, but for some reason that doesn't scare me like it should.

His face drops. "Okay, I'll tell her." He hangs up his phone adjusting himself as he stands looking for my clothes that he threw.

"Blake," he says, which he never calls me. This can't be good. "I had some of my guys keeping an eye on your grandma and they tried. Someone broke into her house and..."

I didn't even hear him say the last words because I could feel the world crashing down on me. It is the same feeling I had when the policemen showed up to my house after my parents' accident.

I heard they have to say the words 'died' or

'dead' and not 'passed away' or 'no longer with us'. I know they have to say it, but it doesn't take the pain away.

CHAPTER 24

Emmett

Blake lays in my bed on my chest, only in my hoodie, emotionless and numb. She doesn't say much these days. I took care of the final arrangements for her grandma, as Blake was the last of the family she had there was no funeral.

The plot next to her parents was open, even if it wasn't I would have made sure they all were able to rest together. People will do a lot for the right amount of money.

"I'm going to make you some food, okay, little lady?" I whisper, kissing her head. I knew she wasn't watching what I put on for us. She was only pretending. It was like she was a shell of a person, just going through the motions.

She doesn't say anything, only rolls off of me. It hurts me to see her so depressed.

Blake was teaching me how to use the fancy espresso machine before her grandma died. But I am not even close to as talented as she is. However, that doesn't stop me from making her her favorite drink.

It typically stays untouched, along with the food.

A pounding knock comes from the front door and I turn off the burner before grabbing my gun. I look at the security camera feed, seeing it is just the cops. I put my gun back in its hiding place. I don't need that on me while talking to them.

"Emmett." Hunter, the first policeman, greets. Alex, the other policeman nods his head at me. I know them from high school and just like me they didn't become muscular until after they graduated.

"You guys need something for the shift?" I imply.

The police department was the first one I started to bribe, so I could run my business. There are a few policemen that use my business for their own pleasure.

"Nah, not today. I'll see one of your boys after my shift though. There is a new Sergeant and given your relationship with Blake Sanders." Alex answers me and I move out of the way so they can do their 'search'.

"Coffee is in the kitchen, kill as much time as you need so it looks believable." I head back to the kitchen to plate up Blake's food. I can only hope that she will take a couple bites of this at least.

"You know I am trying to take an early lunch, Emmett!" Alex yells as I walk upstairs.

"Who's that?" Blake quietly asks, I close the door behind me. I know they won't come in here, but I still want to give her the privacy she deserves.

"The cops." I nonchalantly say.

"Em! How can you be calm?!" Blake says with the most emotion I have seen in the last week.

"Little lady, I wouldn't be very good at my job if I didn't have the police in my pocket." I kiss her worried face and place the food in front of her. "Eat a couple bites and at least a sip of water before you drink the chai."

I need to go to work today. The shop can run on its own, but I have to find the people who broke into Blake's house. I can't be doing that here because if she finds out what I'm going to do to these people, she may try to stop me.

I know it was Charlie who ordered the hit, but I can't go straight after him. I need to go after the people who did the hit first, so that he can drive himself crazy from the fear of when I will come after him.

I didn't shoot him last time. I will not make that same mistake again.

~~~~

"Boss, I found them. It was two petty crooks who owed Charlie money. He agreed to wipe their debt free if they broke into this house. They were instructed to hurt Blake. When she wasn't there, they panicked and killed her grandma." Dean shows me the live video feed of the two men, they were barely hanging on as he had given them a beating. "They were harder to crack than I expected, but when you threaten to cut off a man's penis they will tell you anything and everything."

"They're still alive, right?" I can barely see their chests rising.

"Of course, I figured you would want to handle the rest."

"Boss, your brother is out front." Mia pokes her head in. Dean shoves his phone back in pocket. He likes to hide this ugly part of our business from her. But she has to know what we did to her pimp, so she knows that we aren't good people. No way, she believes that we paid him off.

But Dean doesn't want to scare her away and ruin that illusion.

"This is not the day to try to fight with me, Logan." I bark the second I see his smug ass. It has been difficult watching Blake go through this, leaving me highly irritable when I'm away from her. I feel like I can't do anything to help her. I'm just watching her suffer.

I barely wanted to leave her today with Teddy.

"I'm not here to fight. I heard about Blake's grandma and she hasn't been in class all week. Is she okay?" Logan sheepishly says. His hands in his pocket, trying to not start a fight with me.

"No. She has lost her whole family. She is a mess." I tell him.

"How can I help?"

"Will you make sure Teddy isn't neglecting her? Since somehow you have a key to my house AND know where I live."

"Come on, old man. You're not the only criminal in this family." Logan smirks walking back to his car. "Hey Emmett." He stands behind his open car door.

"Yeah?" I ask.

"You better kill the motherfuckers who did this."

CHAPTER 25

Blake

I am not a risk to myself. I don't need a fucking babysitter. Yet, I have to sit in the living room with Teddy while he forces me to watch the Fast and Furious series. Something about how his childhood crush was this one girl and she's exactly like Mia.

I don't really understand, nor do I care.

"Teddy, how much do I have to pay you to give me something to take the edge off?" I propose. Emmett would never give me anything, but I want to feel something so desperately.

"I like living, so no." He turns his hat around before adding M&Ms into the bowl of popcorn he was eating. Holding the bowl out towards me and I wave it off.

"He would never know that it was you who gave me something. Just something, nothing crazy. I would even accept weed." I beg. I have learned that I like Teddy the best out of everyone. It just feels like he gets me better than the other two.

Mia and Dean seem too locked up for me to befriend them. They have dropped by a couple times since…

Just at the end of the day Teddy is the only one who isn't treating me like I am broken. I know I'm broken. I don't need them to remind me as well.

I do love all of Emmett's patience with me, but he hasn't touched me like that since that night. I may be broken, but I still *crave* for him.

"Have you ever even smoked weed before?" Teddy asks, pausing the movie.

"Yes I have." I lie. Knowing damn well the closest I have gotten to smoke weed is watching Scooby Doo when they get the munchies.

"Bull. Shit." Logan's booming voice comes from the front door. "Good thing Emmett sent me here." He walks over with a bag of food and a coffee. "He instructed me to feed you and only to give you this after you drink some water." Logan hands me a bottle of water.

"So, you are talking to him now?" I ask.

"Only because neither of us trust Teddy in making sure you don't do anything stupid since you're grieving. And I am seeing that we were right as he was feeding you popcorn with candy and you were trying to get him to sell you drugs."

"Are you sure it isn't because the paper portion of our assignment is due tonight and you are worried that I don't have my portion done?" I take a sip of the water. It feels heavy in my throat making it hard to swallow. Everything takes so much energy and effort that I can't handle it. Including this conversation.

"Just if I happened to need to use your laptop would that be in Emmett's room? And is your canvas logged in or do I need to ask you for the log in?"

Emmett

I don't kill people because I have the *need* to. I'm not like Ted Bundy or any of those other freaks. I kill people who have wronged me or the people I *love.*

I was never a particularly religious man growing up, but I have a feeling this isn't helping my case to get me into heaven.

This warehouse used to home me when I would run away from my life at home from time to time. Logan and I would sleep on cardboard boxes to hide from mom's boyfriends when they would decide that they needed to 'discipline' us.

Now it is where Dean takes the people we

need information from.

Dean didn't hold back, following my orders to a t. The two men in front of me have dried blood all over their face, with many parts of their faces swollen. You wouldn't recognize them from afar.

I didn't want to know their names, it keeps me from humanizing them.

"Which one pulled the trigger?" I darkly ask Dean. I don't have to worry about the forensics part of this, as that is what Dean is good at. He covers up what I need him to.

I don't ask questions, nor will he give me the answers.

"The one on the left." Dean hands me an untraceable handgun. I don't care what kind it is, none of that matters to me at this moment. I never go overkill with the gun. I want them to *suffer*. And this time isn't any different.

A butterfly knife is my weapon of choice. I used to have one with no blade since they are illegal. Not that it matters to me about the legality of something.

But one of mom's earlier boyfriends gave it to me. As a child I thought he was the coolest guy ever for giving it to me.

I don't think he knew that it would lead to

this.

"I don't care what you do to the other one." I flip open the butterfly knife. The man was screaming against the duct tape wrapped around his head. Over the years I have learned not to hear their screams.

You don't realize how much power it takes to stab a person until you are there. Going through the layers of skin and muscles shouldn't bring me this much joy. But watching him yell out in pain as my knife plunges into his stomach.

I know Blake's grandma's death was quick and painless. However, they will not receive the same mercy.

No, they will watch as I gut them, begging for me to put them out of their misery. I will cut his hand off, sending it to Charlie. The tattoo on his hand being the only identifiable thing about the limb.

Only then will I put him out of his misery.

CHAPTER 26

Emmett

After killing a man, the first thought that comes to my head shouldn't be how good my little lady looks with her ass out as she lays in my bed with only my hoodie on. And I mean *only* my hoodie.

Yet, I'm coming out of the shower after washing all the evidence away and all I am thinking about is how much I want to fuck that ass, her cunt, her mouth. I just want to fuck her.

If she knew what I did mere hours ago, all the blood I had to wash away, she would not want me to take her virginity. Which is why I have been holding back so much. Why she had to kiss me first, why she had to make the first moves. I refuse to force my life on her.

"I tried to stay up." Blake sleepily rolls over as I slide in behind her. She snuggles into me.

"It's okay. I had some business to take care of." I mummer inhaled the scent of strawberries and vanilla in the body wash that I bought her. She would never ask, but I knew it would make her feel better if she didn't have to use Old Spice 3 in 1.

"Did they deserve it?" She vaguely asks, implying that she knows what I did tonight. I could easily make up a lie that there was a car that needed to be done by tomorrow, but instead I don't.

Blake is the kind of person that makes me want to open up to her, makes me want to spill all my secrets, all the horrible things I have done to survive. Tell her all my hopes and dreams, how I always dreamed of being some kind of English Professor where I wouldn't be making tons of money. But that wouldn't matter because I would be analyzing modern works to classic works, in an academic setting.

I would have a loving wife and my kids would never feel the feeling of starvation. They wouldn't have to worry if the power would be on when they got home, if there would be enough food for both of them.

We wouldn't be rich, but we would be happy.

I want to tell her all of that. Hell, I want to live all of that with her.

"Little lady, I don't do anything unless they deserve it." I kiss her head, loving that I am hearing her voice once more.

I spent hours, days, waiting to hear her speak after the news of her Grandma. I longed for the conversations we would have in my car. How I didn't savor those moments more. How if I could go back in time, I would tell myself to savor the car rides as there would come a day where you wouldn't know the next time you would hear her voice.

Which is why I am savoring this moment and answering her questions, even if I don't want her to know the horrible things I did to those men.

"I asked Teddy if he would sell me something, anything." She quietly admits, spinning the silver ring on my thumb. It's nothing special, something I made myself one day while at the shop when I was first starting out.

"He didn't give you anything, right?" I feel the anger creeping up on me. Teddy is a stupid man, but he can't be this stupid that he would take advantage of my grieving girl.

"No, he said he enjoyed being alive."

"Why did you want…." I let my voice trail off, flashes of my mom laid out on the bed with pills all around her. My fingers trembled as I had to call Charlie, as I didn't know any numbers. I was too young, but his number was on the speed dial on my mom's cell phone.

Charlie said I was smart to call him, that I would have been taken away from my mom if I called anyone else. I didn't want to leave my mom.

Adult me is screaming back at child me that maybe if I was taken away I wouldn't be the horrible and evil person I am now.

"To feel something. I feel so empty."

"*Blake*," Her name coming out of my mouth without thinking, but it came and it came through gritted teeth. "There are so many other ways to feel something."

"Then show me, Emmett. Show me." Blake's ass grinding against my crotch. All my blood and better judgment rushing towards my cock.

"The moment I let go, the moment I let my urges take over I'm never going to be able to stop. I have waited ten goddamn years for you and I will spend the rest of time making up for all the time it took for you to come to me." I growl into her ear, sending shivers down her spine. She doesn't scare away, all it does is make her want me more.

I have wanted her from the moment she was in my car, the moment I smelled her vanilla perfume.

"Let go, Emmett." My dick surged at those words, like everything inside of me had been waiting for her.

Quickly flipping her over, I stare in her green eyes, the flakes of gold throughout has always been my favorite part. But right now, I don't want to stare in her eyes.

Roughly kissing her, she tries for a release, any kind of release she could get by grinding her hips against mine. I hold them down.

"Little lady, you will get that release, trust me you will." I warn as I hold her down. "No underwear?" I feel the heat between her thick thighs, her thighs slick from how much she wanted me.

She shakes her head, biting her lip. The innocence in her face shouldn't drive me this crazy. I must be a pretty fucked up man to see that and think about how much I want to corrupt that innocence.

"What if Logan came up here looking for me? Or Teddy? Or Dean? They would have been greeted with your bare ass, hanging out from under *my* sweatshirt. I can't have that, can I?" I groan, releasing my dick from the confines of my black boxer briefs. I know that I am longer and thicker than most men, by the reactions that I typically get. And this time was no different. Her eyes wide, wondering what she got herself into.

"Please," She moans, begging. And that is all I needed from her.

Her cunt so damn slick, so damn tight, all I have ever longed for has been right here. At this moment I don't feel like the evil man I have made myself into, no I feel like the god in which she believes that I am. She is all mine and I am all hers, and that is all I could ever want in my life.

My hand finds her clit because she is not making it easy to keep me from cumming. It is taking everything in me to make sure she is taken care of first.

Her walls tighten around my cock, making it harder to hold on. She chants my name like it is a prayer, riding the waves of her orgasm. Her nails find my back, keeping me close to her.

She looks so damn beautiful, I was not going to be able to hold on much longer. I waited too damn long for this, so when my balls began to tighten and my control was gone. Grunting to myself, I felt myself losing myself to Blake Sanders.

I felt myself give up a part of me that I have kept hidden for so long. The part of me that allows me to love another person.

CHAPTER 27
Blake

Emmett lays on top of me, showering me with kisses, as he mummers words about how I was such a good girl. He pulls himself off of me at some point, I don't exactly know when. I was already drifting off to bed.

Warm wet washcloth is rubbed against my inner thighs, Emmett showering them with kisses.

"I should've worn a condom. It's been so long, I was too much in the heat of the moment." He apologizes.

"I have the implant." I sleepily hold up my arm, showing him where it is and then pulling him next to me. "Now cuddle me." I demand.

"Yes ma'am." Emmett throws the washcloth to the floor. Crucio emerges from under the bed, crawling into my arms.

What is that saying about how blood doesn't define family?

Because I may have lost everyone, but right now I don't feel alone in the world. I'm still broken, but Emmett is the glue that will put me back together.

I woke to an empty bed, saddening me. Was it too good to be true? Did I just give up my virginity to a man who I thought deserved it, but actually didn't?

Before I could continue spiraling down, Emmett pushes through the bedroom door, arms full of take out bags and a coffee cup in the other.

"I thought I would make it back before you woke up, but the line for coffee was insane." His wide grin sends those thoughts away. "But don't worry I'll make up for my tardiness" he pulls the blanket aside to reveal my naked body, lying between my legs.

This man was serious when he said once he started, there was no stopping. For a while last night I thought I was still dreaming as he laid in the same position, waking me up in pleasure.

"Then what were you making up for in the middle of the night?" I ask, moaning in pleasure and want as he continues to tease me.

"That's making up for lost time. I have so many years we spent apart to make up for."

~~~~~

If this is a dream, I hope I never wake from it. Emmett Grayson Thornton is the kind of man I waited my whole life for. Sharing all of my firsts with him was worth the wait.

He hands me one of his shirts and my now lukewarm McDonald's. I'm too hungry to even wait for it to be warmed back up.

"I feel like I should know more about your childhood." I admit, sipping my coffee and putting my half eaten breakfast sandwich on the wrapper laying in front of me.

"That's because I didn't really have a childhood. I would rather hear about yours." Emmett voiced as he put on a pair of black boxer briefs. The tattoo on his rib cage was older than the rest and harder to make out as he hasn't touched it up in years.

"The first time I felt drawn to you was when I found out about the fact that my dad was not my biological dad. Not that it matters as blood doesn't make family. I mean maybe that's why he spoiled me so much, afraid that one day I would find out the truth and wouldn't want him as my dad. They put me in anything and everything that I wanted. 8 am ballet class on a Saturday and then a 10 am softball practice, my parents didn't mind. They would haul me from place to place. But I can count on one hand the times my dad told me no. My mom on the other hand would have to be the bad guy to keep my dad and I from buying a pony. I know she hated being the bad guy and having to tell me no. I really should have listened to her more when she would say no instead of going behind her back to my dad." I vaguely say. The memories of our last phone call coming back to me.

"You were a child. Children do that all the time. Logan knew that if I said no, if he could find my mom she would typically say yes." Emmett tries to comfort me.

"But I wasn't a child. Not the last time." It has been easy in my life to not have to relive my parent's death. I avoid any and all questions when it comes to them beyond the fact that they are dead. But Emmett doesn't pry, he doesn't try to force me to tell him anything.

Instead, I feel the want to share my stories with him.

"If I could go back in time and tell myself that I didn't need ice cream at that moment and I could have waited until the next day. Or even until they got home, I could have driven myself. My mom insisted that we had ice cream at home, but it was just popsicles. They never found the driver who hit them, they died on impact. The driver was driving a stolen car, probably drunk. They were pulling out of the parking lot when the driver hit them. I assume it was a man, he fled from the scene on foot shortly after. How fucked up is that?"

Emmett holds my hand, rubbing it as I stare off in the distance.

It's sad to think that at almost 21, I have no family in the world. That everyone was taken away from me in the worst ways possible.

"Little lady," He pulls me from my thoughts, his deep voice grounding me. "I know, it seems like life is really fucking you over. I used to think the same thing. And I know it took a lot to share that with me, so thank you for letting me in. I can and I will find the man who did that to your parents and make sure he pays."

CHAPTER 28

Blake

As a woman, you are taught to look at your surroundings, check who is around you. You are taught all of these techniques, so you know if you are being followed.

However, what do you do if you are?

And is it just the paranoia of being a woman? Or is there actually danger there?

The car has been following me for what feels longer than usual. My early morning shift at the coffee shop had just ended and I was heading to the shop to get lunch with Emmett.

I have slowly been going back to my regular schedule. I haven't been back to my house and I ran out of clothes forever ago. But baby steps.

Teddy and Mia were going to go by to gather me what I need, later today. As much as I didn't mind rewashing my one pair of jeans and cycling through Emmett's hoodies, it would be nice to have more options.

Teddy was going to go alone, but he got all weird when it came to the fact that I would need bras and underwear.

I still haven't made it to a single class, but my advisor said I would be able to repeat any classes that I do not pass without penalty because of my Grandma.

I just need to be sure that this car is following me. I make a right turn that I would not need and the car does the same, coming super close to my bumper. I should call Emmett just in case.

He upgraded my stereo, so now I can take calls through it. Which at this moment I am beyond grateful for.

"Little lady, how was work?" He cheerfully answers, the sounds of his shop echoing in the background.

"Emmett." I nervously say.

"What's wrong?" His voice darkens.

"How do I know if someone is following me?" I keep on checking my mirrors, unable to see the driver's face. Their tint is too dark for me to even see through the windshield of their car.

"Where are you right now?"

"Maple and ash." I look at the cross streets that are coming into view.

"Make a left, don't signal. Just make the left and then you are going to blow through the stop sign. Dean is super close to that right now. Teddy! Get Dean on the fucking phone, tell him to tail the person following Blake right now. She is approaching him in less than 2 minutes." Emmett angrily orders Teddy and then becomes more tender while talking to me. "The key is that you don't stop long enough for them to be able to get out of their car. Or worse they may try to ram into you. Dean will not let anything happen to you, little lady. I promise."

I do exactly as Emmett orders, the car behind me trying to catch up to me. "Should I be speeding? I feel like this is where I should not be following the rules of the road."

"You are going to hit a long road soon that will take you directly to me. That's when you should floor it and you don't stop until you get to my shop. Dean should be behind the car. Do you see him?"

I look into the rearview mirror and see another tinted car behind the one following me.

"Does he drive a big car? I don't know the kind, but, like, what celebrities use to escape paparazzi." I press down on the gas, hearing sounds that I should probably tell Emmett about when I get to the shop. But right now, I am just hoping it holds on long enough to make it to him.

"He drives a Jeep Cherokee."

"Em! I don't fucking know car names! Like a SUV type of car!" I ask in panic, afraid that this is a second car that will be used to kidnap me.

"Yes, it should be dark gray."

The feeling of relief comes over me, knowing that Dean is close enough in case of anything. Which is needed as the car behind me tries to ram into me once again. I swerve into the other lane to keep from getting hit.

I can feel the man behind me panicking as we approach Emmett's shop. The dirt road leading to his shop comes into view, his shop is away from the main road. Which makes sense knowing now what he does.

"Blake, I need you to listen carefully. Dean is going to hit the car behind you. As soon as you hit the dirt road, you need to move to the opposite side of the road as soon as I tell you so and brake. You have to trust me." He speaks carefully to me, making sure I understand everything he is saying.

"But," I begin to protest.

"There is no buts, just trust."

"I trust you, Em." I grip my steering wheel and hope that I will not lose traction on the dirt road when I quickly swerve.

"Now!" His voice yells, I swerve, hitting my brakes as hard as I can. The road was wide enough that I was safe on the other side, just like Emmett said.

Dean sends the car in front of him in circles, tail whipping. He quickly gets out of his car with his gun drawn. Emmett, Teddy, and Mia come flying towards us, stopping in front of the now stopped car. They hop out of the car, Emmett running towards my car. Teddy and Mia stand near Dean with their guns drawn.

"Little lady, you can let go of the wheel." He quietly tries to coax me out of my seat. I just begin to cry, the adrenaline of the chase is gone.

He unbuckles my seatbelt and pulls me out of the car, in his arms.

"I got you. I'll never let anyone ever hurt you. Remember that, little lady. Nobody here will ever let anyone hurt you." Emmett carries me to his car. "I even let Teddy drive the Subie, so I could get to you quicker. That extra two seconds it took him to put the car in park, was two too many seconds I would have been away from you."

"You must have been really worried if you

let him drive it." I giggle between my sobs into his chest. He sits in the backseat with me, which he is way too big to be in the backseat with me. But he isn't complaining about how uncomfortable he must be with me across his lap.

"Little lady, I hope you know that I'm never letting you out of my sight after this."

CHAPTER 29

Emmett

I guess my last message to Charlie wasn't enough. That's fine, it's his men he is sacrificing, not me.

That's why I don't feel guilty as I gutted this man who followed my little lady. He gave up Charlie faster than a virgin boy on his wedding night.

Dean takes the heart of the man from me, still warm as I watched this man bleed out only moments ago.

I would deliver this myself, but I can't let Blake out of my watch. I don't know what Charlie has planned, but I will not let him use her to get to me.

If he wants to take me down, then he can come after me.

"Who is watching Blake if you're here?" Dean packages up the heart carefully. We sell to a mailman, so he owes us. Which is good because

Charlie has his house locked down with armed men, if they saw us coming they would shoot us before we even got out of our car.

"Logan, Teddy, and Mia. I figured between the three of them, Mia could handle it if Charlie tried to kidnap Blake again." I pour some hydrogen peroxide on the ground for the dried blood stains. We would have some of the newer guys deep clean this building later tonight.

"So her and Teddy?" Dean beats around the bush.

"If you are going to try to talk to me about your girl issues while you are handling the heart of a man who I just killed, then I am going to need something to drink." I wash the blood off my hands with the hose before stripping down to just my underwear. This is why I keep an extra pair of clothes in my car, you never know when you may have to burn the clothes you are wearing because you had to murder someone.

How do you tell the woman you love that you just killed a man for her? I feel like I should have flowers for that conversation.

"You're right. I fucked it up with her." Dean tapes the box closed and drags the body, along with our clothes to the back room.

"Dean! It's been 3 years! Either make a move

or let Teddy bang the girl you love." I yell, teasing him. He throws an empty bottle of bleach at me. The roar of the industrial furnace is my signal to head home.

"Logan and Teddy got her drunk, so you owe me." Mia meets me in the driveway, I could hear the music blaring. I am pretty sure they are badly singing along to a Queen song.

"Thanks Mia. I can't keep her locked up forever, she won't allow it." I stare at the dried blood in my nail beds. "What do I do?"

"Emmett, you know what I'm going to tell you. You won't know peace until *he's* gone."

I don't know what I expected when I came inside, but Teddy, Logan, and Blake drunkenly filming Tik Toks was not it.

"No, no it is side step, THEN hip sway!" Teddy yells at the other two who can't stop laughing.

"Maybe we will do better if we take another shot." Blake hands the bottle to Logan after taking a swig from it.

"I think you are right, Fire." Logan chuckles after taking a swig. "I could be on Dancing with the Stars."

Fire?

"You would have to be famous or good at dancing to be on that, Ice." *Ice?* Blake giggles, her eyes lighting up when she sees me standing in the living room. She runs towards me, jumping in my arms. "I made ex... es..."

"Espresso!" Teddy yells as Blake is tongue tied.

"Yeah! That! Martinis! I had like 5!" Blake showers me with kisses, tasting like the alcohol she just had.

"Well, don't let me ruin your fun. I gotta shower and I'll come join you guys. I take it that Teddy and Logan will be spending the night." I place Blake back on the ground.

"Yeah! They're going to cuddle in the guest room!"

"As long as they don't join us in our bed, then I don't care how they sleep." I reach for her wrist, pulling her in for one more alcohol tasting kiss.

"Ours?" She mummers against my lips.

"Yes, little lady. Ours."

CHAPTER 30

Emmett

I watch the YouTube video as I attempt to make latte art. It looks like crap, but I'll just drink it or Logan. Logan comes stumbling into the kitchen wearing some of my clothes, as his were covered in vomit by the end of the night.

"God, your girlfriend really knows how to drink." Logan holds his head in pain, sitting at the island in the middle of the kitchen. I slide the latte to him.

"Oh, so what happened to those nicknames you two had for each other?" I open one of the cabinets to hand him some Tylenol with a large glass of water.

"Don't worry, I don't want her like that. She's fire because of her red hair and I'm ice because of my blonde hair. She's deeply and madly in love with you." Logan states matter of factly, no hint of resentment or jealousy. He has always worn his emotions on his sleeves, so it's easy to tell he's being honest.

"Do you want a breakfast sandwich?" I change the subject, Blake joins us in the kitchen wearing my sweatshirt that is so long on her that you wouldn't be able to tell that she has shorts underneath. I only know because my first reaction when I see her is to smack her ass. I know it's barbaric, but if you saw how good she looked you would understand.

"Two, please. God, Blake, how are you not hungover?" Logan grumbles as Blake cheerfully makes her and I lattes with way better latte art. She hums to herself.

"Maybe because I am not old like you two. Em has a hangover if he even sniffs alcohol." Blake hands me my own latte with a heart made out of foam. "And I wasn't even that drunk last night."

"Little lady, I would love to cover and lie for you and say you weren't drunk last night. But you laid on the ground crying about how birds aren't real anymore, so they could never fall in love." I kiss her cheek as a thank you for the coffee. "I have to go into the shop today, so you have to come. You can hang in my office."

"When did I turn into Rapunzel and you are my fake mother?" Blake mopes, sitting next to Logan.

"Does that make me Flynn?" Logan takes a long sip of his latte.

"God, no. You can be Pascal."

"I refuse to be the lizard!" Logan protests.

"And I refuse to let you be the love interest." Blake hits Logan's chest, almost making him fall off the bar stool.

"I liked it better when Logan was leeching off of you for your brains." I interrupt their bickering with a plate full of bagel sandwiches for them.

"I did like it better when he was just a dumb frat boy with a hot older brother." Blake grabs me by the shirt. "Thank you, Em." She pulls me down to kiss her.

~~~~

"How long do I have to be locked away?" Blake asks, around hour 8 of sitting in the shop she wanders out of the office. My head was in an Audi, trying to fix whatever the horrible noise it was making.

People drop all of this money on a car, but they don't know how to take care of it.

"Until I take care of the threat." I grumbled, annoyed that I can't get this car to work and angry that I haven't been able to deal with Charlie yet. Wiping my hands on my coveralls and slamming the hood down with a little too much force. Mia can figure this out for me, my head is too full to find the problem.

"Who is this threat? What does he want to do with me? Nobody is telling me anything, yet I'm the one at risk." Blake jumps on my workbench, making her closer to my eye level. She innocently watches me as I deliberately wipe off my hands on a spare rag before I touch her, not wanting to get grease all over her.

"Charlie. In my line of business you make more enemies than friends. I dethroned him, taking over the empire he built. To him I was always his friend's kid, who he was helping by showing him how to make a quick buck. I was smart, I knew from history how to take down a kingdom. Which he didn't expect. We had an agreement because he owed my mom that he would never mess with Logan. Now, that I have shown that I do have a weakness, he is using it against me. He will kill you, thinking that I will surrender. But he doesn't know the lengths I will go to keep you safe."

CHAPTER 31
Blake

I don't think Em likes it, but I still have bills. So, when one of my coworkers asked if I would work double, I had to say yes. They covered all of my shifts, so I wouldn't lose my job after my Grandma.

Emmett is hellbent on sitting outside of Chili's the whole night if he has to. He has the tracking on my phone, yet he is still worried that this Charlie guy is going to come after me while I'm at work.

"Is he really going to sit outside the whole night?" Claire, the hostess, asks me as we roll silverware.

"Yeah, you know with the guys who murdered my grandma never getting caught," Gotta leave out the detail, that they will never get caught because Emmett and Dean dealt with them. They wouldn't tell me the details, but that their message was heard. "He is worried about my safety."

"He could have at least come inside and ordered some food." Claire is disappointed that she did not get to see Emmett. Everyone has been asking if he would ever come inside, as they would love to have something good to look at.

"I took him out some food during my 30 and we ate together. He hasn't had a chance to read, so he is perfectly content with his book in the car."

"Hey Blake, can you take out the trash?" My manager Brandon asks. Brandon is a younger manager, but it's Chili's. Closer to my age than Emmett's and looked like would be spending Friday nights in a frat house, rather than this Chili's.

"Brandon, I can do it. I'm almost done with my silverware." Claire offers up as her pile was much smaller than mine.

"Claire, you still have to clean the hostess stand. It is a disaster." Brandon reminds her. "Blake, trash and then you can leave for the night."

"I'll finish your side work. Go see your boyfriend." Claire offers, taking my pile as her own.

"I owe you." I happily pull my phone out to text Emmett that I just have to take out the trash and I'm all his. Also adding into the text, that he is choosing dinner because my brain is dead.

The trash in one hand and my phone in the other after hitting send, I push the back door open. A hand is wrapped around my mouth muffling my scream. My phone and trash falling to the ground as I try to attack the mystery person behind me.

"I'm sorry, Blake. I had to." Brandon emerges, kicking my phone away. He locks the door behind him. A wet rag, smelling like chlorine, is pressed to my face. It has a slight sweet smell, which is never shown in the movies.

They also don't tell you that when you are chloroformed, it isn't instant. I am still fighting my attacker for as long as I can. The more I scream the more of the chloroform I'm taking in. Yet, I'm hoping that Claire or Emmett will hear my screams. Someone. Anyone.

But no one does, I'm all alone in the world once again. No Emmett, no Teddy, no Logan, no one. Just me against this attacker.

And I'm no one's pawn, no one's damsel in distress. Like Emmett says I'm his Lady, and I will not be taken down.

CHAPTER 32

Emmett

"No, you cannot eat that. Blake made *me* snickerdoodles, not you. If you fucking eat the last of it, I will murder you and feed your body to pigs!" I yell into the phone at Logan. I'm so happy that Logan is back in my life, even if he won't leave my house and is once again eating all of my food.

I know it is just because his dad has once again walked out of his life, which I should feel sad about. But he needs to learn to cut him off, just like I had to learn.

"Sorry Emmett, you are breaking up. Did you say that I *could* eat them? You are such a great brother. I love you, see you when you get home!" Logan ends the call before I could yell at him.

"Emmett?" One of Blake's co-workers asks through my open window. I am taken back that she even knows my name. "I thought Blake left like an hour ago, so I'm just surprised to still see you here."

"What do you mean?" I look at the tracking

on my phone to see that she is still 'here'. But something doesn't feel right.

"Our manager asked if she would take out the trash and then she could leave. I saw her go out back, so I assumed she came around to meet up with you."

I don't wait to hear the rest of the story, I am running around to the backside of the building. Calling her phone over and over again, knowing it is no use.

She changed my ringtone to the prologue song from the Harry Potter soundtrack, and I followed the melody to under the dumpster. Her phone was cracked, but still in working condition.

The manager was breaking down boxes by the door, the look in his eyes confirms everything. His fear that he has for me.

I pocket Blake's phone before rushing the man, pushing him against the wall.

"What did you do?!" I grit through my teeth, pulling my butterfly knife out of my pocket. I hold the sharp blade against his face.

"I had to. He threatened me." He coughs out. I apply pressure to the knife, it doesn't take much to get him to say more. "H-He said all I had to do was to get her away from you. That's all I did."

I can't kill him, not here. He knows more than he is letting on. Charlie won't care what I do to this guy. He was a pawn, and he has my queen.

Like I've said I don't like to learn names that humanize the person. I don't need that. I threw him in the trunk of my car after taking his phone and zip tying his limbs together.

"He has *her*." I say through gritted teeth, speeding down the roads to my house. Dean answered after the first ring. "He *fucking* has her!" I hit my steering wheel out of anger, trying to keep my composure. But when it came to Blake, I never had that ability.

"Boss, we will find her. We will get her back, but you need to put your want to kill Charlie aside, so we can find her. She needs you right now. Blake is strong, she isn't going down without a fight." Dean tries to reason with me, speaking to me as a friend and not as my right hand man.

"I'm going to lose her." I feel the tears coming down, I never cry. Not that I can't cry, but nothing has ever given me the desire to cry. Until now.

~~~~

"What can I do?" Logan asks after helping me tie Blake's manager to a chair.

"You should stay out of this. I have been

trying to protect you from this life." I sigh, pulling out the man's phone, but he has more than just a face ID or fingerprint to unlock his phone.

For a manager of a Chili's, he has a lot to hide.

"Give me the phone. I'll find out what you need." Logan doesn't wait for me to hand him the phone, he takes it out of my hand running back inside. I follow closely behind, knowing that Dean will be here soon.

And I would kill this man from my anger and we would learn nothing. The pleasure I would get from gutting this man.

I'm going to draw out his death, making it as long as painful as possible.

CHAPTER 33

Blake

Copper pennies, no blood, hmm no, pennies. Wait, don't they taste the same? That's all I could taste in my mouth. My brain couldn't decide what it was as it was still groggy.

"Em." I try to say, but my mouth is dry. My senses come back to me, feeling the pain in my side. I start to remember what happened.

"You poor thing, crying out for your boyfriend. He isn't here, but he will know soon enough what his presence had on you." The man with reddish brown hair had a scar across his face.

"Charlie." I mutter.

"Oh, I kind of hoped you would call me dad." Charlie says. "Your mother, now she was a fighter. The fight she had, the way she tried to kick me off of her. It was what drove me wild, making me want her more even if she didn't want me. That didn't matter. She tried to lie to me, even after I gave her money to deal with the problem that she was not pregnant with my child. She begged for me to stay away from her, but no one ever compared. She stayed hidden from me as long as she could, but if I couldn't have her then no one could."

"What are you trying to say?" I can't wrap my mind around what he is saying.

Charlie steps closer to me, the smell of cigarettes coming off of him.

"I raped your mother and then killed her and your so called step father. Now I'm going to kill you. Is that simple enough?" Charlie hits the side of my head with his gun. "Stupid fucking bitch."

It takes everything in me to stay alert after that hit. But I will not let him end me.

"Emmett is never going to let you live after this." I angrily spit the blood dripping into my mouth right at him. It angers him more, but he holds back from hitting me again.

"You really have more faith in him than you should. He had the chance to kill me, but you made him weak. You will be the downfall to his kingdom." Charlie hits me harder with the gun, knocking me out.

CHAPTER 34

Emmett

I ignore the cries of the man as Dean does what he is good at. I move the squat rack to reveal a fake floor, where I hide my heavy duty weapons. This is the stuff that would get me locked up if it was ever found.

Logan is tracking down Charlie using the manager's phone. I am too focused on the hole in my heart that I have from the disappearance of Blake to understand what he is saying.

"He doesn't know anything, if he did then he would have told me by now." Dean stands over me, blood splattered on his face.

"Doesn't matter. Cut off his hand or kill him. I don't care. He is the reason my little lady was taken and he must pay for his part in this." I slam the trap door closed, moving the mat over it and then my squat rack.

"You want to do it?" Dean offers up the bloody knife to me.

"I'm saving my murderous tendencies for Charlie." I stand up pushing the weapon away from me. "Maybe show Teddy the ropes, have him help you."

"You think he is ready for that?"

"I don't give a fuck. I need Blake back and it was this asshat's fault that she was taken!" I yell, letting the anger take over for me, punching the whimpering man. His begs are easier to tune out than I would like. But right now all I want to hear is Blake's voice.

"I found him." Logan's happy face pops into the garage. "That the guy that gave Blake up?"

I nod, Logan's smiling face is replaced with anger. His cold demeanor chills me as he takes the knife from Dean, stabbing the guy in the stomach, slowly twisting it.

"Fucking coward." Logan spits out. I've never seen him like this. "I'll tell you where they are, but I'm coming with you. She may be your girlfriend or whatever, but she's my friend as well."

"No, you aren't coming." I slam the door behind me, chasing after Logan.

"We are all coming." Mia is sitting at the island in the kitchen cleaning her gun. "So, get your righteous bullshit out of here."

She tosses her now assembled gun to Logan.

"I already called the hospital and told them to expect a guy missing a hand. He won't say a word, so let's go get your girl back." Dean says. "I'll send the boys to come clean your gym."

~~~~

Blake

The sharp edge of the chair rubs away on the rope wrapped around my wrists. It is difficult to be discreet about it with the two men who are watching me and that's not including Charlie.

I don't know what I will do once I get out of the confines of this, but if I am going to die either way, then I would rather die trying than not at all.

"Why haven't you killed me?" I cry out at Charlie, he was smoking a cigarette in the corner.

"Silly girl. Don't you know that pawns shouldn't speak?" Charlie holds the cigarette in his mouth as he shoves a rag in my mouth, wrapping duct tape around my head, so I can't spit it out at him. He takes my inability to speak to put his cigarette out on the exposed part of my thigh that is showing through my ripped jeans. I scream out in agony.

The white hot pain makes me light headed, but then the voice that I love is heard. I don't know which one of my injuries killed me, but I am grateful that I can hear Emmett's voice while in the afterlife.

It's dumb because if I was dead I would hear my parents or my grandma. Which is why I know that this is real. I want this to be real.

"You fucking bitch. This wasn't the plan!" Charlie yells, holding a gun to my head. "I had plans to draw out your death, recording it so that Emmett would know that it was all his fault. But now I have to be quick about it."

I try to fight against him, but he is holding tightly onto me. I use every last bit of energy I have to try to get the last part of the rope to rip so I can hit him. If I can get a punch in then I know I can fight my way out of this.

"Blake!" Emmett's voice echoes through the empty warehouse over the sound of gunshots. I can't yell back at him and tell him that I'm here and that I'm alive.

"I want him to watch the consequences of his actions." Charlie holds me by my hair, tugging as hard as he could, so I have to look up at him. I hate that I have the same eye color as him, I hate that I share similarities with this man.

All this struggling allows for the rope on my wrists to finally break. Emmett and Logan come guns blazing, they look injured but they aren't stopping.

"Look at the family reunion. This will be even better." Charlie mocked, like he has the upperhand in this situation. I want to use my new found freedom to hit him, but if I time this wrong I'm going to die.

"Charlie, your men are dead. It is 5 vs 1, even with how dumb you are you have to realize that you are out numbered." Emmett calmly says. Out of the corner of my eye I see Dean with a sniper rifle lining up his shot.

Dean can see that my hands are loose and I see him nod to me after I motion that I could hit him, allowing me to escape. It's a slight nod as he steadily holds his position.

Trust. Like how I trusted Dean and Emmett when the guy was following. Like how Emmett trusted them to watch over me.

If he is giving me the okay, then I have to.

I hit him in the crotch as hard as I can, he bends over in pain and with my legs still tied to the chair I jump as far as I can.

Emmett runs to my side as soon as Dean makes his shot. He throws his gun to the side, ripping the tape away from my face and pulls the rag out of my mouth.

I hold tightly onto him, not wanting to let go.

"H-he killed my parents. H-he raped my mother." I cry into his arms, making little to no sense. He just holds me, not moving. The world keeps moving around us, as his team works to cover up the crime scene and they assess each other.

However, Emmett and I just stay here silently holding each other. I don't know who cut my legs free, but I used the freedom to wrap them around Emmett's waist.

He stays quiet, holding onto me. I listen to his heartbeat, letting the noise of the world disappear.

CHAPTER 35

Emmett

I placed Blake on the toilet, we haven't said a word since we left the warehouse. Just holding onto each other as tightly as we can. I turn the shower on before carefully taking off her shirt.

I run my fingers lightly over her injuries, angry with myself. I didn't want to overstep, so I stayed in my car. I should have overstepped.

She winces in pain and a part of me dies on the inside, knowing she's hurt because of me. I couldn't give her stitches, I can tune out the sounds of the cries for help of the men I murder, but I can't disassociate from her cries.

Dean didn't say anything when I couldn't touch the needle to her, he just took over for me.

No one really knows what to say after that.

Undressing Blake should not feel this somber, but I am holding back the part of me that wants to rip off all of her clothing like she was water and I was dehydrated in the middle of a desert.

I don't want to hurt her more than I already have. My own damn brother is getting stitched up because of me. I never wanted this for any of them.

Even with my house being full of people as everyone recovers from what just happened, I feel alone and angry. I can hear them downstairs working their way through my liquor cabinet once again. As much as a drink sounds so good at this moment, I want to be right here with Blake.

I let the water hit Blake first, trying to not hurt her as I wash the dried blood and dirt off of her.

"I'm sorry," I mummer, holding the bottle of strawberry vanilla body wash in one hand. I want to throw this bottle out of anger, anger for what I let happen to Blake. Instead, I hold it so tightly that the bottle may break.

"You didn't hurt me." Blake quietly says.

"But…"

Blake cuts me off before I can spiral with a kiss, I haven't known the right moment to kiss her. If I should have kissed her when I finally had her in my arms, or when she was in the car with me. Just like our first kiss, she doesn't wait around, she takes control.

"I love you," I whisper against her lips, holding her close to me.

"I love you too." Her voice is quiet and small. "I want to dye my hair, I need to change it." She abruptly says.

"What color? Teddy can go to the store or I can make an appointment for you." I want to be supportive during this time for her. If she asked me for a million diamonds to get her through this, I would find a way to get that for her.

"He gave me my red hair. I want it gone." She blankly says. Is there a therapist that I can blackmail, so she can be honest about everything that happened?

I can do that for her. I'm not a good person, I can't give her white picket fences. But what I can give her will be worth more than that.

~~~~

Teddy and Blake had too much fun dying her hair, I think they enjoyed destroying my bathroom. Hair dye has to be easier to clean up than blood, right?

"Is she going to be okay?" Logan asks, handing me a water bottle. Her laughter from the other room brings me joy even if it is because of Teddy.

"I'll make sure. Do you happen to know any psychiatrists with some skeletons in their closet?" I jokingly ask the second part.

"Rhett Burns. Graduated when I was a freshman, he was in my frat. Do you want his school records and his public records? Great psychiatrist, horrible online poker player." Logan pulls out his phone, texting me this guy's files.

"Should I ask?"

"What did you always tell me when I was young? It is better for your safety if you don't." Logan slyly smiles.

Blake emerges from the bathroom with towel damp hair, her fiery red hair now replaced with a dark blue black artificial color. It changes her demeanor. She's no longer my little lady, she's my queen.

EPILOGUE

Blake

2.5 years later

"'Based on the passage above, if genetically modified crops were to be banned, what could be the largest negative impact to humans?' I don't remember high school being this difficult." Emmett reads out loud from the laptop in front of him, sitting on the ground of the now empty guest room.

"You were also in high school a million years ago." Logan answers, building the crib that would be taking over the room that had basically become his over the years. However, Emmett and him had finally started on building the house next to ours.

"You're the one who wants to have your GED before the baby comes." I sit in the overpriced chair that I saw in passing and said it would make a good nursing chair. I've learned not to say things in passing because Emmett will go back to buy it, not caring about the price.

"Well, if I am going to retire from the crime

world, then I need to have some kind of degree." Emmett closes the laptop.

"Does a GED even count as a degree?" Logan teases when in actuality we are both very proud of Emmett for going back to get his GED. "Also, what are you even going to do? It isn't like you can put on your resume that you ran a drug empire for the last twenty years."

"You really think that people don't lie on their resumes? I also have enough powerful people in my pocket that I could get any job that I wanted." Emmett hits Logan in the back of the head before coming over to kiss me. He plays with my red hair. The therapist I have been seeing for the last 3 years got me back to a place in which I feel comfortable to have my natural hair once again.

It'll never be easy to look in a mirror and see all the things I inherited from the man who raped my mother, but I have to remember that he isn't my father.

We don't plan on telling our daughter the truth about her biological grandfather until she is older. There is a lot about both of our families, we will have to keep it a secret from her until she is older. However, she will have the best chosen family she could ever ask for.

"Where's your ring?" Emmett looks at my empty ring finger, the semi permanent indent is still there outlining where my engagement and wedding band once stood.

"Your daughter has made it impossible to wear anything. My fingers are too swollen now and it was either taking it off or cutting off my finger from lack of circulation." I complain, I hate the empty feeling. Emmett and I got married in secret a year and half ago, it wasn't like we were ashamed. But neither of us wanted to have a big celebration. One bribed priest and two strangers later, we were married and off to lunch to celebrate all in an hour.

"It's okay, I'll just get you a temporary one. I have to let people know you are *mine*."

"I'm 30 weeks pregnant, the size of a fucking house and you are one of the most feared men in town. I don't think anyone would ever dare to flirt with me." I remind him. I know he said that he and Logan were small as children, but this is just proof it was the lifestyle they had that made them small. Because his, yes his since it is *his* fault that I am this size, child is possibly going to have to come early since she is so big.

"Emmett, I was reading that book you gave me. So, when I'm delivering the baby..." Logan begins to tease.

"No fucking way is your brother seeing my vagina while I give birth. I want a real doctor." I cut him off, the emotions making the words be way more harsh than I would like it.

"Well, I guess Dean could do it, he would be better than Teddy at it." Emmett continues to tease.

"I'm going to murder the both of you. I hope you know that." I threaten and the boys begin to laugh.

"Little lady, if you wanted to kill me, I would provide the gun." Emmett kisses the top of my head.

"I'm about to graduate in forensic science, I could murder you and make it all look like an accident."

"The true art is murdering someone and making it seem like they disappeared off the face of the earth with no trace. Don't worry, I'll show you all the ways your classes were wrong."

This life isn't a fairytale, not like how they show in Disney movies. Emmett isn't my Prince Charming, he would be seen as the villain of the story. His lifestyle isn't for the weak.

But that's okay, I didn't want Prince Charming. That seems boring.

Maybe Cinderella would have had more fun in the underworld than in a Kingdom. At least, I know that I am.

The King of the underworld sounds way better than Prince Charming anyways.

The End

AUTHOR'S NOTE

Blake and Emmett's story isn't quite over. Follow more of their story in Dean and Mia's story, 'Chancellor'. How did Dean become the right hand man of Emmett? How did Dean save Mia from her old life? How did Mia become Dean's one that got away? Did Dean drive her away forever and into Teddy's arms?

All of those questions are answered in the next book.

ACKNOWLEDGE MENTS

First off, thank you to everyone who has read my story and made it this far.

I want to say thank you to my best friend for reading absolutely everything I write, including Draco Malfoy fanfiction. Thank you Alexis for designing the cover and editing everything I have ever sent you.

And a big thank you to my husband for supporting me with my addiction to reading the absolute worst kind of smut that led to me wanting to write. And also, thank you for educating my ex mormon self about basically everything and anything I needed to know for this book.

Thank you to my niece for designing Emmett's tattoos and agreeing to not reading any of my books because I used to change your diapers. We grew up more like siblings than aunt and niece and I refuse to let you read my books.

And thank you to the long list of friends who spent time looking at different covers.

A big thank you to my 4th grade classmates that read my superhero book that I wrote and never finished, yet that didn't stop you guys from being my biggest and earliest hype men.

And my 8th grade friend group that loved my story that I wrote about us in the zombie apocalypse and I misspelled one of my friend's name in every single line mentioning her. She didn't have a hard name, I just couldn't spell.

Thank you to everyone, thank you for encouraging me and hyping me up.

CHANCELLOR

By Alana Keli'ipule'ole Trumbo

Edited by Alexis Cotant

CHAPTER 1

Dean

3 years ago

I should be thanking Emmett for taking me in when I had nothing, no one. Giving me a new identity, so I become untraceable with no strings attached. I could run away, I could take all the money I have made from him and run.

I have never stayed in a place this long, making friends has never been my thing. He put me on the streets, slinging dope like I had been doing for years. The only difference is that he makes sure I have three square meals and a roof over my head at the end of the day.

No one is this nice with no strings attached. Which is why I should run.

There is no such thing as an honest drug dealer.

He said it was time I moved up, time to make some good money. Emmett explained to me that these men don't care how much they have to pay for what we sell because all they care about is discretion. Some of them are so powerful that we could ruin their lives by letting their identity out.

This bar prides themselves in how discreet they are, all the NDAs everyone must sign to even think about stepping foot in this place.

The only reason I am even let into a place like this is because I am providing the thing they want.

Escorts, hookers, women of the night, whatever the hell you want to call them are paraded around, like these ugly rich men could actually land one of them.

A man in an expensive suit slides a stack of hundred dollar bills to me. Sometimes they are nervous and ramble, other times they act like I don't exist. As if I was a drug dealing vending machine.

I hand him an 8 ball, counting the money as he walks away to make sure he didn't stiff me.

Fifteen hundred for an eighth of coke. They don't realize how much they are overpaying, nor do they care.

I don't have to worry about having someone watching my back in this kind of location, I'm all alone. I actually prefer this.

I still have a gun on me. I don't trust any of these rich assholes.

"Just whatever you have on draft." I tell the bartender, handing over a bill from my wallet. I don't have any debit cards, they make it too difficult to run when I need to.

"You're new." A girl to my right tells me, her beautiful golden brown hair catches my eyes. The dark red mini dress clings to her figure, highlighting her curves. For a moment I'm speechless, I hate this feeling.

"Got rid of the other guy." I simply say, taking a drink of my beer to give my brain time to catch up as it is still focused on the incredibly gorgeous woman next to me.

"Angel," She held out her hand to me.

"Dean," I'm still getting used to this new name. I shake her hand before I see an older gentleman calling her over. "I don't think your 'date' appreciates you talking to me."

"He's not paying me enough tonight to have any kind of claim on me. Hopefully I see you around, Dean." She flashes her smile at me, before heading back to the table with the man probably triple her age.

"I understand you are new around here, so I should warn you. That's the governor's choice of a girl, so you should stay away. He hates when other people talk to her." The bartender warns me.

"Fuck the governor." I take my drink away to the table in the corner that I had taken as my own. The governor may be powerful out there, but he should be afraid of me. I could ruin his life a lot easier than he could do the same to me.

~~~~

"Beer?" Emmett holds one to me, it is close to 3 am. But no one sleeps in this kind of industry. He had just opened up his mechanic shop, some kind of front for us. He made me go to trade school before I was able to work the streets, so I could work in this shop with him.

I don't know why he does this, why he is treating me this way.

I shake my head, placing the band of hundreds on his desk. His office was still under construction with the boxes full of books taking up most of his room.

"How was it?" Emmett takes the rubber band off the money and places it in the bill counter behind him.

"Rich snobby assholes who don't care about who I am as long as they get their coke fix. I don't know why you sent me there. Anyone with half a brain could work in this location." I said angrily.

"Do you need to fight someone to get this anger out? Or Are you just fucking sexually frustrated?" Emmett snapped. "Go fucking punch someone or get laid, but you need to knock this attitude off." Emmett's anger radiating off of him

"So, you want me to pay one of those fucking ladies at the bar because you believe that'll keep me from being an ass?" I yelled.

"If that's the only way you can get laid, then yes. Now get out of my fucking office. You're back at the bar tomorrow night and you better be in a better fucking mood when I see you or you're in the shop every day until you change your attitude." Emmett opens the safe that's under his desk after giving me my cut from the night.

I take my cut and storm out of the building before getting on my bike, it roars to life. It is nothing special, barely even classifies as a working motorcycle, but I don't want special. I want functional.

CHAPTER 2

Dean

"Hi, how can I help you? Can I interest you in an 8 ball of coke?" I put on a fake customer service voice equipped with a fake smile when Angel approaches my table. Her dress is much like last night, except it is black. She has a sparkly new necklace on, that is probably worth more than the both of us.

"What the fuck is wrong with you?" Angel laughs, taking a seat at the other side of the rounded booth, sitting across from me. She was sipping on a ruby colored drink.

"My boss said I needed to either get laid or punch someone, so that my 'attitude' would change." I scoff at the outrageous comment that Emmett had, sipping on the now lukewarm beer. I hate to admit that I left it sitting there while I looked around for Angel.

"Ahh could poor Dean not find someone to fuck?" Angel teases, flashing her bright white smile that makes me melt. Makes me want to forget about the argument I had with Emmett. Well, if you could consider it an argument…

I'm used to the yelling and throwing of objects when it comes to an argument. So, I guess ours was more of a discussion.

"He told me to pay one of you to have sex with me if I had to." I answer as a middle aged man comes close to me, holding out his hand for a handshake. Except his hand has cash in it, so I shake his hand sliding the baggie in his hand.

"One of us? Do you think I'm a hooker?" Angel angrily asks.

"I-I mean the bartender said…" I begin to stammer as she breaks out into laughter from my embarrassment. I could even feel the blood rushing to my cheeks. "You're fucking with me, aren't you?"

"Yes, I am. And for a small price I could even fuck you." Angel continues to tease.

"Nah, I like knowing the actual names of the girls I sleep with. I also don't want to steal you away from the governor." I take a long drink of my beer, trying to catch my breath from that scare.

"Jay likes to think that I'm his, but he is very mistaken." Angel looks at the door, like she is waiting for someone to show up. That is when the man she is waiting for walks in, a man that looks like the Godfather himself walks over to us.

"Angel, you should not be with one of Emmett's boys." He threatens, his Boston accent is quite thick. This man probably thinks he is some pimp version of the Godfather. He angrily pulls on her, almost pulling her to the floor with the amount of force.

"So, you know who I work for," I step closer to him, pushing him away from Angel. "Then you should know what I do to men who place their hands on pretty women. If she wants to enjoy a drink with me while she waits for one of your many wealthy clients then she will. Understand me?" I begin to twist his hand. It takes a lot to break a bone, but at this angle, it becomes as easy as breaking a twig.

"Y-yes." He whimpers out, that doesn't stop me from breaking his wrist. A message must be sent. He cries out in pain, the bar becomes silent as this man runs out of the room.

"I don't think I need to get laid anymore." I say with a smile on my face, sitting back in the booth like nothing happened.

"He's going to be pissed for days about that." Angel sits back down, finishing her drink. She seems unphased as well, this is what our line of work does to a person.

"Fucking good," I hate to admit that Emmett was right, I did need to hurt something.

"Well, that'll save me from telling you which one of these girls you should fuck tonight." Angel orders two more drinks for us. I wouldn't have taken her suggestion anyways, unless it was her.

"Why do you do this job?" I ask as the second round arrives for us.

"Why does any girl get into something like this? Father figure issues. Seventeen foster homes before I was twelve."

"Twenty-three and a couple of group homes before I was fifteen, that's when I had enough." I admit. Something I actually haven't told anyone before. You don't really learn how to make friends when you are constantly being moved around.

"I knew I liked you for a reason. You're just as fucked up as I am. I didn't make my break for it until I was sixteen, I could usually take what the foster dads were doing to me. But something about that last one, I had enough. The wife was yelling at me to get out about how I seduced her husband, blah, blah, blah. I took my trash bag of clothes and never looked back. That's why now I make people pay me for sex because if the wife catches us and yells at me, at least I can take his wallet on the way out and still get paid."

"Fuck, I got kicked out at fifteen when I started fighting the foster dads back. They can hit me, but once I beat the living shit out of them, they get angry." I hold my beer up. "Cheers to fucked up childhoods."

"Cheers!" Angel smiles. We spend the rest of the time until her client walks in talking about how we both made it to this town. How we would steal for a decent meal, walking as far as our legs would take us to get us away from our hometowns. She would exchange favors for rides, whereas I lucked out to get a few nice truck drivers. And ultimately how we both ended up in our jobs.

It felt nice to have someone who related to me, someone who understood me.

"My client is here, will you be here tomorrow night?" She looks at the door as a well dressed older gentleman in a suit walks in.

"As long as my boss finds the change in my attitude worthwhile, then yeah I will."

"Dean, not everyone will turn on you at a drop of a hat. Give that boss a chance. You gave me a chance and you knew me for far less than you knew this Emmett guy for." Angel grabs her half empty drink, she smiles at her client.

"Well, it's easier when you are a beautiful woman and he's not you." I let the beer do the talking, in the moment not regretting those words that came out of my mouth.

Angel doesn't say anything, just letting the blood that rushes to her cheeks do the talking.

CHAPTER 3
Mia

My shoebox of an apartment has nothing to show for me, except a mattress that lays on the floor. I have enough money to buy furniture, but I need to have enough to get away from Nathan.

Dean may have dealt with him last night, but I just know he will find a way to add the hospital charges to my debt. Dean doesn't need to know that. By his reaction last night, he would be livid.

I rinse out my one bowl, crushing up some top ramen in it before filling it with water and putting it in the microwave. My landlord left the microwave for me when he saw that all I had was a trash bag full of clothes.

He must feel bad, but he doesn't question much as we barely even have a lease. I pay him way above the asking price in cash and he leaves me alone.

I don't know how to cook, so unless my clients decide to take me out to eat I am either eating takeout or Top Ramen.

However, there aren't many places that are open at 3 am, so Top Ramen it is.

I can't fall for Dean, I have known him for two days. He is just fun to talk to, but he is the first person to hear the real story of how I got into this industry.

Most clients want to hear some fake story they can pretend to be a part of. Some want me to be their friend's daughter, their sister in law, some random chick in the bar that is hitting on them.

The governor likes for me to pretend to be his own daughter's best friend. I know, gross and sick. However, he pays for it.

He likes that I'm his dirty little secret, I like that he tips me well for my discretion.

I stuff more money into the fake box of noodles before putting it back in my empty cabinet.

I'm so close to being able to leave this place and start over. It does mean leaving Dean, but again I just met him. He doesn't even know my real name.

I will get enough money, so I can look for my sister and get out of this industry. That is the goal, remember that.

~~~~

Instead of deciding on which dress my client would like the most, I chose a dark green one. It will go nicely with Dean's eyes.

"So, your boss liked your new attitude?" I smile as I see the fluffy light brown haired boy sitting in his usual booth.

"Well, he didn't yell at me to go get laid and didn't threaten me with working in the shop instead of coming here, so maybe his heart doubled in size like the grinch." Dean pushes a ruby colored drink towards me. "I asked the bartender what you drink, soda water with a splash of cranberry. Not much of a drinker?"

"Waste of money to have a vice." I sip on the drink, I don't usually take drinks from people. Not even my own clients, there is no one to trust.

"Everyone has a vice, you have one."

"Don't do drugs, don't drink, I don't like the taste of coffee, so really no caffeine unless I really need it then I will have a cola. So, no vices." I list off, my clients even think that I'm always drinking vodka sodas with a splash of cran. The bartenders and I have an agreement since I always make sure my clients tip them very well.

"Your vice is sex." Dean leans across the table, he's not wearing an expensive cologne that all the other men in this building are wearing. It smells more like Old Spice, not that I'm complaining. I like it more than anything anyone in this building is wearing.

"Dean, if you want me to sleep with you I can tell you my prices." I tease him. I love watching the blood rush to his cheeks as he blushes from my comments. How he chokes on his beer from my comment. Dean always takes to his beer when he needs a second, so I like to play this game where I try to see how quickly I can make him finish his beer.

He doesn't know that he's playing this game, but that makes it even more fun.

"I've seen your clients, I don't think I can afford you." Dean finally says once he regains his composure.

"Um, how much for what you're selling?" A nervous man stands next to Dean. He is one of the youngest men in this building.

"What are you wanting?" Dean's voice darkens as he goes into business mode.

"I don't know man," The man sheepishly says.

"Maybe, this isn't for you. Stick to alcohol and weed. Stay away from men like me." Dean ends the deal without selling. Most dealers would have seen this naive man and taken advantage of him. The man runs off, more afraid of Dean than he would like to admit.

"Why didn't you sell to him?" I raise the question to him.

"No reason to take advantage of someone who looks so young that he probably can't even grow a beard. If he is truly desperate then one of my other guys will probably sell to him, but maybe he will actually listen to me." Dean answers.

"You look too young to grow a beard." I tell him. He would look good with some five o'clock shadow. Not a full beard like a lumberjack.

"Darling, I'm older than you." He leans across the table once again and I want to lean across and kiss him. That wouldn't look good for my brand, though. They can't see me kissing the dealer for free.

I do reach out to touch his face, "Maybe so, but your baby face says something different." I let my hand stay there for a second too long before I remember that my client is about to show up, this wouldn't look good.

"So, you like facial hair on men?"

"I would like facial hair on *you*." I say before walking off to meet my client by the door, not saying bye to him or asking when he would be here again. I need to hold some restraint when it comes to Dean.

I need to remember what my goal is.

Made in the USA
Columbia, SC
05 December 2022